WAKING THE LEVIATHAN

WAKING THE LEVIATHAN

WAR OF THE DAMNED™ BOOK FIVE

MICHAEL TODD   MICHAEL ANDERLE
LAURIE STARKEY

Beta Readers

Dorothy Lloyd
Tom Dickerson
Dorene Johnson
Diane Velasquez
Timothy Cox
Sarah Weir

JIT Readers

John Ashmore
James Caplan
Mary Morris
Kelly O'Donnell
Angel LaVey
Peter Manis
Micky Cocker
Larry Omas
Paul Westman

If we missed anyone, please let us know!

Weapons Consultant
John Kern

Proprietor
Spurlock's - Henderson NV

Editor
Lynne Stiegler

Three Weeks Earlier

Katie was nervous as hell.

They had come to the end of Korbin's and Stephanie's tour of the base, and now it was time to have the talk she'd been anticipating and dreading in equal amounts. Katie led them into the conference room across from her office. Her two old friends took their seats at the expansive oak table and looked at Katie, their expressions patient but curious.

Katie didn't know where to begin. She still hadn't come to terms with her feelings about taking their demons in the first place. She'd done it for them, but it had been a huge personal sacrifice to lose them both. She felt halfway guilty for bringing them back in and all-the-way guilty for being so happy they were back.

Pandora cut in on her thoughts. *You are overthinking this. You heard Stephanie, they were going to volunteer. At least now you get to protect them.*

True. I just couldn't bear it if they were killed because I took their protection.

Did you ever think you would class demons as "protection?"

No. Except for you. I have to keep Korbin and Stephanie safe, P. They're too important to me. To the whole team.

Stephanie smiled, sensing Katie's discomfort. "This place is amazing. Whoever put it together did a fantastic job."

Katie smirked. It was just like Stephanie to put her at ease. "The designers were some of my closest friends." She winked at Stephanie.

Korbin chuckled and took Stephanie's hand. "Sounds like we were involved, sweetheart."

"That really doesn't surprise me," Stephanie replied. "When we were on the tour, I saw my style and taste everywhere I looked."

Katie nodded and smiled warmly. "This entire base was designed by the two of you after we had to leave our last base. You guys knew that it was hard for the team to lose the only home we had. You put your money, your time, and your hearts into making this not only a fortified base but a home for us all."

Korbin shook his head in wonder. "This is just all so strange. I don't remember any of it." He gave Stephanie a questioning look. She shook her head. She didn't remember any of it, either.

Katie sighed. "I wish I could give you back your memories." Korbin looked at her sharply. Katie raised her hands defensively and shook her head. "As far as I know, I can't. But maybe I can shine some light on all of this? It's the least I can do after... Well, everything."

Korbin gave her a comforting smile. "Calvin told us what you did, and why."

Stephanie nodded emphatically. "We don't hold it against you, Katie. You did it out of love."

Katie swallowed the emotion that welled in her throat at Stephanie's sincerity. "You have no idea how relieved I am to hear that. Calvin told you some things, but there's a lot that I wanted to say and didn't get the chance to. You two are more than *like* family to me, you *are* family. Letting the two of you go was one of the hardest things I've ever had to do. Bringing you both back in was another." She looked down at her hands on the table. "You took me into the group, and you gave me something I didn't think I would ever have again after becoming Damned. You didn't just train us, you took care of us while we took care of the demons. When you two fell in love, it broke my heart to see you both hold back in case one of you didn't make it through a mission. But neither of you voiced a word of complaint because that was the life we lived."

Stephanie hesitated for a moment. She looked at Korbin, and something passed between them. After Korbin nodded slightly, Stephanie asked, "Will you tell us about it?"

Katie smiled. This was exactly why she had taken their demons. Seeing their love made it a bit easier for her to tell the story. Only by a little, though.

She closed her eyes and steadied herself. "Our last battle together was really fucking bad. They've gotten worse since, but that one...that one made me take action to protect you both. So many people died. So many. We lost some of our own. Too many in a small family like ours." The faces of the fallen flashed through her mind. She let them run and took a moment to appreciate that Korbin and Stephanie were not among them. She opened her eyes and smiled at the two of them. "After the fight, you were sitting together under a blanket, sharing a meal and just appreciating a quiet moment together. I walked over and asked you if you wanted a future together, something better for the rest of your lives than just war and death. I think I already knew what the answer would be. When you told me that you did, my demon and I pulled your demons out of you. With that, all the memories from your time as Damned were taken too."

Stephanie frowned and scrutinized Katie. "I definitely remember you, just not the way that you are now."

Katie grinned as she recalled some of the happier memories of their past. "I met you before you were Damned, but you didn't fully understand what we were or what we did until you were Damned yourself. With all those memories gone, that would leave you, what? Your brother and a few short memories of me...and Joshua, maybe?"

Stephanie's eyes lit up at the name, but she held her questions for the moment.

Korbin took a deep breath and glanced at Stephanie with a smile. "It sounds like you gave us back our lives. You gifted us an opportunity to spend some *very* quality time together. For that, we thank you. It's just so strange to not be able to remember anything."

Stephanie flashed Korbin an excited look. "Especially since we were fighting and kicking demon butt. Perhaps that's why we felt so strongly about finding out how we could help after Incursion Day?"

"It wouldn't surprise me at all, Stephanie. You two have the biggest hearts." Katie reached over to the seat next to her and grabbed the box that was waiting, then opened it and took out a file. She slid it across the table to Korbin with a nod. "This is just a drop in the ocean. Notes and files you kept while you were the leader of Korbin's Killers. I thought maybe having some of the facts in your own hand would help you feel more connected."

Korbin opened the file and skimmed the first page. The brief overview of his career as a Damned mercenary was unfamiliar. He turned the page and was confronted by the bios of the Korbin's Killers team members. He wished he could remember them, especially the ones who were marked as KIA on his watch. The fact that he couldn't didn't sit well with him.

Stephanie sensed Korbin's pain and leaned into him. She linked her arm through his and read along with him. Katie waited patiently as they flipped through the pages. They both were surprised when they came to the information on themselves, Calvin, Katie, and Damien.

Korbin couldn't deny what he was seeing. He had handwritten the notes on the bios. He shook his head as he recognized the sheer scale of this operation. He let out a long breath as it hit home that he had not just been a part of that one operation, but had been an integral asset in the war against the demons.

Katie patted Korbin's hand. "Look, I know this is a lot to take in. I'm going to give you some time to go through the files. The boxes lined up along the wall are all yours; I had them pulled from storage. Maybe something in them will help jog your memories."

Korbin and Stephanie smiled and thanked Katie, and she stood up and made her way out of the room. Before she closed the door, she took another look back over her shoulder at the two of them. She felt guilty for disturbing their peaceful lives, but it was safer to keep them close. Not that their safety had been her only reason for bringing them in. They needed all hands on deck in this war, and the loving couple at that table had a level of badassery all of their own.

She closed the door and set off down the long empty corridor. The base deep beneath the Nevada desert was quiet. Almost too quiet.

Katie hated that she was responsible for Korbin and Stephanie losing their memories. When she had exorcised them she'd thought that the new memories they would make together would make up for the pain and hurt of the past. Now that they were back, though, she realized those lost memories were an important part of who they were.

Katie couldn't stop thinking about it. Pandora had to have something to tell her. *There's got to be a way. There is something we can do to get their memories back.*

Pandora spoke more kindly than usual. *I wish I had a magic cure for it. Pulling demons out wasn't a demonic creation, we just know how to do it. As you might imagine, we don't really like being pulled from our bodies.*

One thing I've learned through all this is that if there's a way to do something, there's a way to undo something. Even if there's only one person that knows how to do it. Katie plopped down in the nearest chair. *What a fucking day.*

Pandora scoffed. *Yeah, you'd have to talk to that stick-up-his-ass, Gabriel. I can just see it now. "Excuse me, but can you go find my friends' memories and put them back in? I know it's, like, against all the rules and everything, but I'm Katie Golden Tits, and I want it to happen."*

Katie snickered. *You would think that after all this time, I would get something out of this deal, aside from angels and demons plaguing me.*

Pandora let out a soft chuckle-snort combo. *Oh, you mean like fame and fortune? What about the ability to save thousands of people's lives and look fucking good doing it? Sometimes I think your head is bigger than mine, but then I remember that your head is my head, so it makes sense.*

I'm not trying to be that way. I'm not even asking for personal gain. Katie sighed and rubbed her face. *I just think that if it's possible and it's for the betterment of others, why would an angel tell me no?*

Because angels are complicated. I keep telling you, they're not as sweet and innocent as you think they are. That is all marketing, sweetie. The angels' idea of Justice has nothing to do with doing what is right, and not everything they do is good for humanity in the short-term. You have to understand, they have worked this way for eons. They don't usually focus on any single person. You are one of the few exceptions—and that's only because you are serving their purpose. They are usually focused on the greater good, which means keeping the Earth under their control. Sure, in the end, their actions save lives, but the only real difference in the way angels and demons operate is that we demons are at least upfront about what we want. When it comes down to choosing a side, it's all a matter of context.

Katie rolled her eyes. *I'm on mankind's side, and I'm on*

Korbin and Stephanie's side. In reality, what do I have to lose by asking? The worst he can say is no, he can't or won't do it. Katie hated to think Gabriel might say no, but she was forced to.

Reality was a bitch, no matter *who* you were.

Pandora pulled Katie from her thoughts. *Oh yeah, and we all know how much you like it when somebody tells you no, especially when you* know *they can do something. Next thing we know we'll be fighting angels* and *demons. You gotta pick a side, sweetheart.*

Katie smirked, knowing that was a bunch of bullshit. *I don't have to pick a side. I picked mankind's side, so all the rest is just schmoozing to get the tools I need to make sure mankind survives this war. I can figure out the rest when I get there. I'm pretty sure whoever sent these angels—the big man in the clouds —knows damn well I'm not some good churchgoing girl. I'm a warrior.*

Does this mean you're going to ask him?

Katie's face hardened, and she pounded her fist into her hand. *Damn straight—if I can get him to come down and talk to me. He probably already knows what I'm going to ask.*

Pandora sighed. *Oh, joy. I'm so fucking excited! I just can't* wait *to meet that twat again.*

Katie snickered and opened the door to her room. She found Pandora's overreactions comical. She locked the door behind her and started to get changed. *What is it with you and this guy? You absolutely cannot stand him. It's like you and Gabriel were previously married or something, and you just don't want to tell me about your bitter breakup.*

Pandora gagged loudly. *Are you fucking kidding me? The mere thought of having sexual relations with that dry as dust, stalky fucksack makes me want to throw up inside you. I cannot believe that you would stoop to that level. Seriously, Katie, even I wouldn't sink that low.*

Katie put up her hands and laughed out loud. *Okay, okay. I get it. You like Gabriel, and you don't want to admit it. That's fine with me. Keep your secrets.*

Katie chortled as Pandora continued to babble on about how disgusting Gabriel was. She slipped into some comfortable pants and a T-shirt. She took a breath and pulled a box from her closet and set it on her bed. She opened the lid and pulled out a couple sets of old clothes that belonged to Korbin and Stephanie. They were their favorite attire to lounge in, and she had held them back when the rest of their belongings had gone to storage as something to remember them by. After they were done going over stuff in the conference room, Katie had something a little less stressful planned.

If Korbin and Stephanie were going to come back for real, Katie wanted to welcome them back the same way she had said goodbye—with love and acceptance. What better way to do that than to have some family time?

Katie's Killers might not be as big as Korbin's team had been, and things were a lot more complicated these days, but that wasn't going to stop her from making sure that her team knew they were a family.

They were all in this together.

She folded up the clothes and smiled. She spritzed Stephanie's with a little bit of her old body spray just to help things along. Afterward, she headed to the common room to let everyone know that they would be watching soaps in about an hour.

Timothy snapped his fingers. "Excuse me, but girl, you

know I'm not going to miss out on one of your famous popcorn-and-soap-opera nights! It's been *too* long." Hands on his hips, he stared expectantly at Joshua.

Joshua shrugged. "What? Of course, I'll be there. It's been like forever since we all did this. I'm not going to miss a chance to hang out with Stephanie and Korbin, even if they don't remember us."

Katie nodded. "Good, let's make them feel as much like family as we possibly can. After all, Korbin started this family to begin with."

Timothy rolled his eyes. "Of course, we'll be missing Damien and his intellectual comments about our soaps. He just *had* to go off and save the church."

Katie snorted, trying to hide her amusement at Timothy's reaction. "Give Damien a break. We all deserve to do what we feel is best. He is living that, and I respect him for it."

"Oh sure, sure." Timothy laughed and lifted an eyebrow.

After gathering the troops, Katie made her way to the kitchen and started to prepare her special sugar popcorn. She went all-out and made a batch in every color she found in the cupboard, then mixed them together to make rainbow corn before filling the bowls. When Katie was done, she stood back and smiled at her work. She felt at home for the first time in a long while.

Stephanie rounded the corner into the kitchen and leaned against the doorframe before Katie had even noticed. "What smells so good in here?"

Katie jumped, surprised by the welcome intrusion. "Oh! Hey!"

Stephanie smiled. "I got tired of looking at the notes, so

I figured I'd do a little exploring. I could smell the popcorn from down the hall."

"It's actually perfect timing. I was just about to come and get you guys. It's family night since we're all here. We get together and watch soap operas and eat sugar popcorn, and pretty much just laugh and talk the whole time."

Stephanie grinned and popped a piece of popcorn into her mouth. "Mmmm, yummy. I love that idea, although I don't know how much Korbin will love soap operas."

Katie raised an eyebrow and smirked. "You'd be surprised how much he got into them before."

Stephanie's eyes widened, and a mischievous look appeared on her face. "Oh yeah? This is definitely something I'm going to give him hell over."

Korbin walked into the kitchen and kissed Stephanie on the forehead. "Who's giving me hell over what, now?"

Stephanie laughed. "Katie was just telling me how you enjoyed your soap operas back in the day."

Korbin narrowed his eyes at Katie, then shook his head, chuckling. "Apparently Katie and I are going to have to have a talk before she goes blurting out more of my past. I have to admit, it's weird that every time I see the soaps on television, there's just something inside me that wants to watch them. Maybe it has something to do with this strange gathering you guys have."

Katie snickered and handed Korbin a bowl of sugary deliciousness. "I wouldn't be shocked. Come on, everyone should be in there by now. They get cranky when I withhold the popcorn."

Everyone gathered in the main room. Stephanie and Korbin sat on the couch, oddly enough in the same place they had always sat. Timothy was in one of the armchairs, Katie took the end of the couch, and Calvin and Joshua spread out on the other furniture.

Katie looked at them all and her heart filled with a warmth that she'd missed. She smiled and picked up the remote and searched through the guide to the last episode they had watched, one from right after Korbin and Stephanie had gone. She pressed Play and sat back, then looked at the others again.

Well, isn't this sweet? Pandora tried to sound sarcastic, but Katie could tell she found comfort in the family reunion.

It might not be the same as before, and things may have changed a lot, but I will always think of these people like my family. That includes you, Pandora.

Pandora sniffed and cleared her throat. *Yeah, well. Whatever. I just want to see what happened to that whore Josie and the ten lovers she couldn't keep her hands off when the gates to hell were open.*

From what I've heard, she got angel wings.

Why do you always have to ruin my life?

Katie snickered and sat back to eat her popcorn. Things might've been awkward when Stephanie and Korbin had first arrived, but having them there was exactly what she needed.

2

A dark blanket of storm clouds unrolled over New York City, obscuring the late summer sun. Lighting forked over Central Park and was closely followed by deep peals of thunder from the quickening storm.

It was a big one. Sheets of rain crashed onto the streets of New York and set the ever-present trash and debris afloat. In no time garbage had clogged the storm pipes. All along the city blocks, black umbrellas bobbed up and down as people continued to weave their way in and out of the foot traffic. They were making their way to work, school, or their next tourist attraction.

The doorman of Katie's building looked at the concierge, who was standing in the entryway of the apartment complex. "It's one hell of a storm out there, huh, Joe?"

His boss gave a flippant wave to tell the doorman he was done with the weather. "We get these storms at least twice a year and let me tell you, the streets weren't made for flooding. Cars will be splashing our guests for the next week, even if the rain stops this afternoon. It makes for one hell of a mess in here."

The doorman chuckled and took a step toward the front doors. He skidded on a wet spot but deftly windmilled his arms to regain his balance. "And apparently, marble and moisture don't mix well."

His boss smiled and shifted his eyes to the doors as two men approached. Both were dressed in long black trench coats and black fedoras. "Question these fellas. I've never seen them before, and with the onslaught of people trying to get Katie, none of us can be too cautious."

The doorman saluted his boss and straightened his jacket. He opened the door and stepped out before the men could step in, keeping the door open behind him so his boss could hear. He could already feel the tension coming from them. "How may I help you, gentlemen?"

One of the two men looked up with a fake grin. "We're here to visit a client of ours."

The other man moved forward, an air of irritation in his voice. "We would appreciate if you didn't make us stand out here in the rain. If we could have had our car pull straight up to the door, we would have."

The doorman glared suspiciously at the men for a moment, noticing their expensive shoes and ostentatious watches. It was obvious that these men had money, but so did almost everyone else in New York City. Big deal. "And what floor will you be visiting today?"

The friendly guy flashed the doorman a crooked smile. "We were hoping you would be able to help us with that. We're here to see Katie, and we weren't sure if she was on the fourth floor or the sixth."

The doorman smiled condescendingly. Like he had not heard *that* one before. "We're not permitted to give out that information. I'm sure if you are expected you could give her a call, and she can give you the information."

The angry one pushed forward, trying to get past the doorman into the building. "I don't think you understand. We are important people. I promise you're going to regret it if you don't let us through."

"I can promise that the two of you will regret it if you don't stop making threats," the doorman warned, standing his ground.

The angry man removed his hat and shook it furiously, splattering water all over the doorman. "I don't know who you think you are, but we'll make sure that you will never work in this town again. And that doesn't necessarily mean we'll make sure you don't get a job, if you catch my drift."

The doorman squared his shoulders. Water dripped from the tip of his nose. "I'm sorry, gentlemen, but you'll have to call Ms. Katie to get the information. I can promise you that she will understand my reluctance to allow two men I've never seen before through to her apartment. Two men who don't even know where she lives."

The angry one reached for the doorman, and his eyes flashed a weak red. "Now, you listen here…"

The doorman grabbed his walkie from his pocket and thumbed the button. "Security, I have two gentlemen at the front door making threats. They are trying to get in uninvited to bother one of our residents."

"Ten-four, we'll be right up," came the reply from the walkie.

The two men stepped back, angry as hell that he'd called security on them.

Both men were livid at this point. Even the friendly man had dropped his mask of civility. "If you don't call off security and let us through, I'll make sure you don't get home tonight."

The angry one leaned in close, whispering, "You want to see what we do when we're mad at somebody?"

The doorman smirked. He wiped water from his face and leaned against the doorway with his hands in his pockets. He nodded along as the two jerks threw out threat after threat, none of which fazed him. It wasn't that he was overconfident or that he wasn't scared of being injured, but he knew he was safe when a situation had anything to do with Katie. He had gotten to know her pretty well, just as most of the other staff in the building had. When she found out what was going on, she would make sure these guys never did it again.

The doorman's eyes flicked up and over their shoulders, and his smile changed to a lopsided grin.

This pissed off the two men to no end.

"What the fuck are you smiling about?" the angry one asked. "We're serious about this."

Both men realized at that moment that the doorman wasn't even looking at them, but was instead looking behind them. They each had a sinking feeling in their gut that they knew exactly who was standing behind them.

The doorman's face twisted into a snarl. "You were saying? What's the matter? I thought you were *serious*."

One of the men grabbed the other by the wrist and shook his head, and both men turned slowly on trembling knees. Their arms dropped to their sides, and their eyes opened wide in surprise.

Katie flew toward them in the pouring rain, wings stretched wide. Her furious wingbeats creating a hot wind that swirled around the two men. For a moment they could only focus on her blazing red eyes. It wasn't until she was almost on top of them that they realized she had two of the gnarliest guns either man had ever seen, both raised like she was offering them a terrible gift.

The doorman darted inside, closing the door behind him. "Oh, man, it's going to suck to be you in three…two…"

THUD!

The concierge looked up from his book, barely showing emotion. "From the look on your face and the amateur percussion session outside, I'm assuming Katie came back."

A couple of screams and yelps filtered through the door and someone banged on it a couple of times, then there was a wet crunch and a protracted groan. The doorman shrugged and gave a crooked smile. "Yeah, and she heard everything they said."

The concierge peered at the door and grimaced. "Well, maybe they shouldn't have come looking for her. It's not like the whole world doesn't know how dangerous she is. Stupid to even *think* about fucking with that woman, if you ask me."

The doorman glanced at the elevator as it dinged. The door opened, spilling a half-dozen security guards into the lobby, weapons at the ready. They stopped when they saw the flurry of wings and flailing limbs outside the doors, then lowered their weapons and watched.

The concierge nodded toward the door and lifted an eyebrow. "I think she's got this one. Grab two of those towels out of the cabinet. I'm sure she's going to need them after this."

A few minutes later, the noise trickled off. The door opened and Katie stepped into the lobby, her wings now retracted. Water streamed down her clothing and from her boots to form a puddle on the floor underneath her.

The security guards stood there for a moment, shocked, holding the towels as the doorman and concierge giggled quietly.

Katie looked up with a huge smile. "Well, that was a good time, wasn't it? You think I might have one of those towels?"

The head security guard looked down at the towel and back up at her. "Oh, yeah. Sorry." He stumbled over himself to get to her.

Katie took the towel and dried her face and neck. "Sorry I took your fun away for the afternoon, guys."

The guard straightened, gathering his wits, and gave a fake yawn. "It's okay. The show was worth it."

Katie held out the now-soaked towel and frowned at the puddle under her feet.

The security guard raised an eyebrow and looked at the other guys. "You know, you might just want to strip down because of your wet clothes and stuff."

Pandora purred. *Oh, they want to play?*

Katie smirked. "You gentlemen have a robe? And a few more towels?"

Confused, one of the younger security guards looked around. The concierge directed him back to the closet, and the young man ran over and came back with a huge, fluffy robe. He had the grace to blush when he handed it to her. She winked lasciviously and undid her weapons belt, then raised her arms and called to the guards, "All right, boys, hold up your towels."

The guys held up their towels, and she stripped while the storm crashed outside. All they saw was the splash of bright red polish on her toenails peeking out. She kicked away her sodden clothing and pulled the robe over her shoulders, and after she knotted the tie around her waist, the guards lowered their towels. There she was, standing barefoot with her clothes in a pile by her feet.

Thunder crashed hard outside.

Although the guards jumped at the sound, Katie didn't take any notice. She took one of the towels and rubbed it over her hair, then dropped it on the floor and stretched her arms over her head. Inside, Pandora chuckled, loving it when she took control of a situation like that.

Katie's eyes sparkled red to blue as she lifted the towel in the air with her foot and kicked it to one of the guards. "You'll get those, won't you, boys?

The head security guy nodded fervently. "Of course. But not before we've cleaned up, ma'am."

Katie grinned, her dimples deep on her cheeks. All the guards melted and let out a collective deep sigh like a weird, perverted chorus of fangirls.

The elevator dinged again, and the door slid open. She inclined her head toward the guards and flowed across the marble floor barefoot, her hair swinging down her back, and her weapons belt in her hand. She stepped inside and winked at the dazed guards as the elevator doors closed.

The men just stood in the lobby, unable to talk or move for several moments. The doorman shook his head and went to grab a mop to clean up the wet puddles on the floor. He found it comical that the guards' reactions were what they were, but he wasn't going to embarrass them any further.

The head security guard started with a sudden realization. He looked up at a security camera tucked into a corner of the ceiling. He knew full well that the whole thing had been caught on tape. He leveled his gaze at the other guards. As he spoke, he pointed his finger at each one in turn. "There better never be a copy of this video released anywhere, or you won't have to worry about Katie. I'll get you first."

One of the guards put up his hands in surrender and laughed. "You don't have to worry about me, boss. My wife would get me before you ever had the chance."

Another of the guards followed suit, nodding dramatically. "The way my mouth was hanging open, I'm pretty sure none of my friends would ever let me live it down. You don't gotta worry about me."

The head guard cleared his throat and tossed the rest of the towels to one of the guys. "Katie's important. Not only are we responsible for her security here where she lives, but we're also responsible for making sure no one knows exactly *where* she is. That video could put her and the rest of us in danger. I'm sure none of us want others to see us drooling over her. Even more so, none of us want to be attacked by demons. Let me hear you all say it—that video never leaves this place."

They all agreed, including the concierge and the doorman. The secret was safe with them. No one would reveal where Katie was or what had happened.

Whoever those two men were, they had rushed off, most likely without the demons who had been hiding inside of them. They were lucky they had been standing outside on a public street. Otherwise, he was pretty sure Katie would have killed them right where they stood. He knew she was a force to be reckoned with, and he wasn't going to do a damn thing to cross her. He was only concerned for her safety and that of the other residents of the building. Having Katie here put their lives at risk.

As for him, he could imagine a lot after a brief glimpse of heaven.

The rumbles of constantly-erupting volcanoes deep within the bowels of hell mirrored the thunder occurring topside. However, the demons were used to it. The chaos was just part of the background for them. They would have found it jarring had the constant seismic activity ceased. Above the landscape of bubbling lava and screaming souls, Moloch and his sidekick Baal were enjoying an early afternoon snack.

Moloch grabbed one of the swishing lizard tails from a bowl, the chocolate melting on his large talons. "The volcanoes are overactive today. His Majesty must be feeling feisty."

Baal crunched down on one of the lizards, and the creature's tail flipped back and forth out of the corner of his mouth. He slurped it up and swallowed, nodding. "From what I've heard, the recent antics of his wife have left him a little bit out of sorts. Then again, it's not like I blame him. She's acting like a complete fool. Imagine, working *with* your meatsack!" Baal cracked up at the idea.

Moloch let out a deep chortle. "You think by now he would be used to her antics. It's not like she was some perfect demon when he met her. Now she's wearing that angel, and she thinks she's invincible."

Baal shook his head. "She's strong enough to fight either of us, and Lucifer can't go topside without all the angels descending upon him. She's found her playground. Unfortunately, she's become attached to those idiots on Earth. But she isn't invincible—we both know that. Between the weapons the humans have created and the protections that angel bitch gives her, she appears way stronger than she actually is. Take those things away, and she's a regular demon just like you and me. Kill her human and send her straight back to hell? Piece of cake. I'm sure his Majesty would *love* to take a strip or two from her hide."

Moloch slammed his hand down on the desk, trapping a lizard that had almost made its way out of the bowl under his claws. He picked it up by its tail and dangled it over his open mouth, savoring the slight stink of fear. He dropped it, and his teeth came crunching down. Blood squirted out of his mouth and ran down his chin. He thought about what Baal had said but shook his head. "Getting rid of those two won't be easy."

Baal leaned back in his chair and lifted one of his dark, furry eyebrows. "Let me ask you a question, Moloch. You've attacked some of the biggest cities in the world and killed some of the most important humans on Earth. Why haven't you gone after the weapons yet?"

Moloch waved dismissively and shook his head. "T'Chezz already tried that and failed. He didn't even get close to the weapons maker, much less figure out where all the weapons were being created. Even when he found their base, they managed to get out and get their weapons to safety without breaking a sweat. After that, the weapons industry exploded."

They sat there stewing for a moment in silence, then lifted their heads and blinked at each other. Moloch sat forward and slapped his hand against his forehead.

Moloch shook his head. "I'm a fucking idiot. *T'Chezz* tried it! I should be banned from eating kittens for a week. I can't believe I let that moron and his half-hearted efforts persuade me that something couldn't be done. He wasn't capable of sucking the soul out of a baby, much less hatching a plan to capture the human weapons. Yet here I was, thinking it was impossible because that moron failed."

Baal leaned forward and patted Moloch on the shoulder. "Don't be too hard on yourself. It's like watching a train wreck—you just want to jump in and eat all the burning bodies before they turn to ash. You aren't thinking about the fact that there's a much better way to do it. We definitely need to look into the weapons situation again, though."

Moloch wiped his chin and eyed the last chocolate-covered lizard in the bowl. "I agree. If we could get control of those weapons, they might be the key to fighting back against Katie and Lilith. She may be a demon, and Katie may be an angel-human hybrid, but those weapons will kill just about anything—including humans. The Damned wouldn't know what hit them."

Baal bellowed loudly, Moloch almost instantly joining in. "I'd love to see Lilith's face when she plummets back down to hell!"

3

Katie sat back on the couch in her apartment, put her feet up, and let out a deep huff of contentment. It wasn't often that she had the luxury of relaxing in her yoga pants and an oversized T-shirt. Her hair was still wet from earlier, but it would soon dry. The adrenaline from kicking those two idiots six ways from Sunday and then stripping in front of the security guards kept a smile on her face. She had definitely become more assured over the years, and what did she have to lose? She could have a little fun when the mood struck her. She was one of the Damned. Her demon was the wife of Satan. On top of that, she was apparently part angel.

Although she had to admit, being the bad girl was a lot more fun than playing the angel.

Pandora cackled. *Damn right it is*!

Katie smirked, but before she could say anything her phone buzzed on the table. She picked it up and wrinkled her nose when she saw the general's number on the screen.

Katie answered playfully, hoping it was good news. "Hey there, General. What can I do for you today?"

"Katie. It's always good to hear your voice."

Katie recognized his tone straight away. "Uh-oh, sounds like you might need something."

The general chuckled. "I forget that you like to get down to brass tacks. I know I've already asked twice, but I just have to ask one last time. Are you sure you're not willing to do a 'hearts and minds' tour?"

Katie sighed and banged her head on the back of the couch in frustration. "I'm more than sure. In fact, I'm so adamantly opposed to a hearts and minds tour that I can't even recognize the request you're making. It's like you're speaking Latin right now. I really don't understand why you want me to do one anyway. You know I'm not the kind of girl you want schmoozing, kissing babies, and shaking hands with all those jerkoffs. I *promise* it wouldn't be pretty."

The general snickered. "I know. I'll admit, I had to agree to ask you one last time in order to get two of my senators off the phone call. You know how they like good press when it's getting close to election season."

"I feel like it's *always* getting close to election season, even right after an election." Katie rolled her eyes, already picturing the banners and signs plastered along the roads.

"That's very true." The general paused meaningfully. "While I have you on the phone, I do want to have another meeting with you, but this time I would like to go someplace different."

Pandora was confused. *Someplace different? What the hell does that mean?*

My best guess? Probably somewhere he knows isn't bugged. These days, I can't even go into a public toilet without worrying about someone listening to me pee.

Pandora shivered, thinking about the last public toilet they used. *In New York City, I'm pretty sure you were more worried about real bugs than surveillance bugs from demons.*

That is true, my friend. Very true. Katie laughed, turning her attention back to the phone. "Sure. You order a chopper, and I'll bring lunch."

The general sounded nervous. "I'm not exactly sure what you have in mind."

Katie laughed. "Trust me."

Pandora whooped. *You know what you should tell him we will do? A Ropes and Binds tour. That way, I can tie up some of those scrumptious men in uniform whose minds you keep promising to blow. If you're not gonna do it, I might as well. Although it's less their minds I'm thinking of blowing and more—*

You've been so damn frisky since our time with Brock.

Pandora shivered again, only this time with a smile. *What can I say? The man packs a mean sausage, and knows what tastes good.*

Oh, my God. Can you be quiet for just like five minutes?

Pandora ignored her. *Well, he isn't dead, and it's been forty-eight hours, so I'm calling the Vagina of Death a conspiracy theory.*

Forty-eight hours is not long enough to call it a conspiracy theory. And it's not like I think my vagina is killing them, just the fact that I'm both an angel and a demon.

"So, are we good, General?" Katie glanced down at her watch, ready to get off the fucking phone.

"We are good. I'll send you a text when the chopper is on its way."

"Perfect." Katie hung up, but Pandora wasn't done.

Okay, spill it. What the hell are you up to?

A mischievous grin moved over Katie's lips. *Nope. You have to wait, just like the general does. I promise it's gonna be a whole lot of fun.*

Why do I not believe you, even for a second?

Katie smiled at the name on the screen the next time it rang. "Katie's door-to-door demon slaying, no demon too big or too small. How can I help you?"

Calvin smirked. "I'm glad to see you still have a sense of humor."

"It rears its ugly head from time to time, but usually Pandora sucks it out of me."

Pandora sniffed hard with excitement. *Tell my black Superman he needs to bring his body back to New York, pronto. Someone needs to keep you under control.*

Katie half-groaned, half-snorted. "Pandora thinks you need to come back and keep me in check."

Calvin scoffed loudly. "Please! I couldn't do that even when we worked on the same side of the country. What does she think I'm gonna do? *She* can't do anything, and she's in control of your *body*."

Katie wrinkled her forehead and emphatically stuck her finger in the air. "Uh, she is *not* in control of my body—let me just make that perfectly clear. If she were, you would see a whole different dimension to me. She would probably *add* dimensions, too. I'd turn up to a briefing one day and be so top-heavy I'd fall over. I wouldn't put it past her."

Calvin laughed loudly. "That is definitely true. In fact, that's one of the top signs I've put on my list to make sure you haven't been taken over."

Katie nodded and laughed along with him. "That would definitely be one of them. So, what's up? Everything good with the team?"

"Yep, working like clockwork. I was actually calling to let you know that I have the bandwidth to come to New York if you need me."

"Oh, yeah? What about your girl? She's a good one, and I don't want you to go and piss her off."

Calvin snickered. He knew she didn't want him to leave, but he wasn't going to tell Katie that. "No. We agree she needs to finish her schooling, but it just so happens that she's thinking about transferring to New York after this semester."

Katie grimaced, thinking about her time in college. "Not UNLV?"

"Ah, nope. She told me there was no need for her to be in a place that was hell on Earth three months out of the year."

Katie chuckled. "Smart girl. Though if I remember correctly, it wasn't all that terrible. Actually, let me take that back. Now that I know about the world and what's happening in it, you couldn't pay me to go back to that school."

Calvin lowered his voice just a tad. "That's what I'm saying. She's gotten a taste of the real world, and she doesn't want to spend her time in a place like that if she doesn't have to. She does love the idea of coming to New York, though, and I don't mind it too much, considering you're there. I know that even if I'm not around, she'll be safe."

"That's me. But yeah, of course, I would have her back. You know that."

"That I do. Well, I'm going to let you go. I've got a lot to take care of out here. Just wanted to call and check in."

Katie grinned. "It's nice having a big brother."

Calvin tried to keep it light. "Don't get all mushy on me. I'll talk to you soon. Let me know if you need me."

"You know I will," she replied.

Katie hung up and stood there for a second, smiling at the empty screen. In reality, it was beyond nice to have someone act like a big brother, and Calvin fit the mold perfectly. Now that things had slowed down and Korbin and Stephanie were back in action—kind of—Katie was feeling more like herself every day.

Angie walked around the corner into the living room, carrying a DVD case. "So, I picked a movie, mostly because I like the extras."

Katie shook the thought from her mind and looked at Angie, excited. "Sweet. Which one is it?"

Angie held the DVD case up and shook it from side to side. "It's *Batman*, the Michael Keaton version."

"Nice. I like Christian Bale as Batman. He's probably my favorite, but I think it's important to start with the classics. Of course, I don't mean going all the way back to the 1943 Lewis Wilson version or anything. I just mean the newer movies."

Angie took the DVD out of the case, walked over to the

television, and stopped, fiddling with the case. "I completely agree with you. The *Batman* movies have definitely gotten a lot darker since the Michael Keaton days. I guess I like both versions, the funny and fantastical of the old ones and the seriousness of the new ones."

Katie rolled her eyes and snorted. "Of course, we can't forget about the new*est* one."

Angie groaned, throwing her head back dramatically. "Lord, the age of Ben Affleck. Actually, he didn't do all that terribly. I just think I hate the Batman versus Superman saga. I really wanted to enjoy it, but I swear, after an hour of watching a plot that could have been resolved by a simple conversation I just fell asleep. Twice."

Katie popped a handful of M&Ms into her mouth from the candy dish on the coffee table. "Agreed, but I think if Pandora's gonna watch *Batman* she needs to see the Michael Keaton before she sees the Bale. Then the Affleck if she really insists, and only if we're going to watch the whole cycle so she can get context on the brood-fest."

Angie put the DVD in the player and pressed the Close button, then plopped down on the couch next to Katie. "I got some info on the testing going on with Timothy's system."

Katie looked at her excitedly. "And?"

Angie grinned. "It's going freaking *phenomenally*. We're on track to get our full price if he keeps it up for another sixty days."

Katie clapped her hands for joy. "Fantastic! So, everything's been on point?"

Angie swallowed a gulp of her soda and nodded. "The cops, with the right weapons, were waiting for the portal nine times out of ten. On the tenth, they got there so fast that they could help people to safety before the gate even opened. It's pretty much a win."

Katie leaned back on the couch and put her feet up on the coffee table. "Perfect! All right, let's begin the *Batman* saga."

The movie started, and Angie flipped off the lights. The silhouette of Gotham City came onto the screen, and Pandora oohed and ahhed as the camera panned out to frame the dirty and dark reaches of the metropolis. *That looks like my kind of city.*

Katie just smiled.

Pandora sighed. *Tragic death of the parents. It always starts like that.*

Pandora watched excitedly as Batman knocked a few junkies on a roof around, throwing one through a door and dangling the other over the edge of the building. Katie couldn't help but laugh at the old-style special effects, but Pandora was more than entertained.

"I'm Batman," Michael Keaton rumbled, starting the movie with a bang.

Pandora shrieked inside Katie's head, causing Katie to grimace. *Holy shit! "I'm Batman." That's perfect. I want to be a fucking vigilante superhero!*

Katie rolled her eyes. *We already are.*

Hell, you're right! I'm a fucking superhero. This is amazing. Why didn't you introduce me to the superheroes before now? All these men in latex and rubber... Wait! Kajesus!

What? Katie was almost too scared to ask.

Is that a nipple on that armor?

Yeah, made out of rubber. Katie thought it was both funny

and a bit strange that Pandora was so hooked on super-heroes all of a sudden.

Dude, I'll give up one week of donuts if you allow me to do one night of superheroine antics...with wings!

Katie bit the inside of her cheek and rolled the candy around in her hand. *Well...I don't know.*

Pandora whined loudly. *Come on.*

Okay, under one condition. You can only do it if you can get the wings out and back in on your own. I don't want us to be switching or something and have the wings disappear. That shit would hurt.

True. Not to mention it wouldn't be very impressive at all to faceplant from thirty feet up at the feet of the criminals. That would be slightly embarrassing.

Angie looked at Katie and raised an eyebrow, knowing something was going on inside the woman's head. Katie glanced back at her and rolled her eyes. "Apparently, now we're not just demon fighters. We're superheroes."

Angie couldn't help but laugh. "Hey, that's what every-body thinks about you and the rest of the teams anyway. Maybe I can make you a sweet mask to wear or something else superhero-y."

Katie twisted her face in exasperation. "God, don't say things like that. She'll take you up on the offer."

Angie laughed loudly, already picturing Katie with a cape.

The wind blew wildly around the deserted area just beyond the neon lights of Las Vegas. Sand and trash whipped through the air, tumbled over the sidewalk, and scattered into the street. Down one of the dark, deserted alleys, a swinging gate creaked open with each new gust, then creaked back shut as it subsided.

There was a loud snap, and in the center of the brick wall, a portal opened. Moloch stepped out of the steaming-hot portal and allowed it to shut behind him. He knew the humans were tracking him somehow, and he didn't want to give them any reason to show up there.

He ducked out of the alley, closed his eyes, straightened his back, and cracked his neck from side to side, then took a deep whiff of the fresh, cool Earth air. A gust of wind blew the dank sour-piss smell of the alley into his nostrils, and Moloch reveled in the scent, slowly letting the air leave his lungs. When he opened his eyes, he looked around. No one was watching. At least, no one except the two people he had come to see.

To the right, their hats tipped low, two men stepped forward. Their black boots sloshed through the oily water on the cracked asphalt. Moloch stood tall, his voice deep and bellowing. "You came."

One of the men took off his hat and hesitantly stared up at Moloch, the light from the adjacent window revealing the fear in his eyes. "We told you we were believers, Oh Great One, and we told you we would do whatever you bade us do."

Moloch grinned menacingly, displaying his long, pointed teeth. "Excellent. A lot has happened topside that I don't like at all. I want control of you humans, but I keep getting shafted by your technology."

The other guy swallowed hard and took off his hat,

stepping up beside his friend. "I can understand that. The military is constantly improving on the technology they received from that Katie merc. It's even been hard for *us* to keep up with."

Moloch snarled, and the sound forced the men to take a step back. "I'm going to need you to pay a little bit more attention to what you're doing. More importantly, I need you to take more interest in what *they* are doing."

The first guy cut his eyes to the other man in an accusatory look, then turned back to Moloch, putting his head down and looking at the ground. "Whatever Your Greatness requires. We're at your service."

"I'm tasking you with finding out if the military has a base for manufacturing these weapons," Moloch told them. "If they do, I need to know exactly where it is and who is in charge."

The guys looked up at Moloch worriedly. "Everything we've heard is inconclusive. No one actually knows where the manufacturing is done. Well, almost no one. Obviously, *someone* has to know to put in the orders, but their bullets and weapons don't even come with an identifying stamp on them."

Moloch lifted his large clawed hand to his face and flicked his talons against one another. Sparks shot from them as they touched, and his red eyes slowly raked over them. The two humans cleared their throats and stared down at the ground, shaking with fear.

The first guy could barely control his fear, and his voice quivered with every word. "Of course, it's important. We'll find the information for you."

Moloch waved his hands, rending reality and tearing

the portal back open. "Excellent! As soon as you know, contact me. You know how."

The guys blanched as Moloch disappeared into the portal and gagged on the hot sulfur wind that blew out from hell. Their stomachs turned as they watched the portal waiver and snap shut. They put their hats back on, no longer needing to hide their place of employment.

The print on their hats read, DSS. Domestic Security Services.

In other words, they were mercenaries.

4

It had been two days since Katie had introduced Pandora to the *Batman* series. In those two days, they had managed to watch every single movie, including the Christian Bale ones. Katie secretly thanked her lucky stars that they had not had time to dive into the Affleck films and all the strange side stories that went along with them.

That morning, before the alarm had gone off and before Katie had even thought about opening her eyes, Pandora was on the move. She had already made plans to continue watching the series, even though Katie assured her she wouldn't like them. She was hooked, and that was all there was to it.

Pandora shouted loudly, knowing she would wake Katie up from her sleep. *How can you sleep right now?*

Katie groaned and pulled the covers over her head. *Because it's early in the morning on a Wednesday. That's how I can sleep.*

You know I'm inside your head, right? Pulling the covers up isn't going to help you much. I just can't stop thinking about

Christian Bale as Batman. Our Funday Monday movie marathon was exactly what I needed.

Katie mumbled cuss words for a moment, knowing full well Pandora wasn't going to let her out of the conversation. She was obsessed. *Keaton was Monday, and he was just as good as Batman.*

Not even close. Keaton got me interested, but Bale makes me want to get boned by that Batdick. And don't even get me started about wanting Bane and his venom wang.

Katie pulled herself up and leaned against the headboard, letting out a deep sigh. *This is not morning conversation. And how the hell can you be hot for Bane and still want to be a superhero?*

How can you have all these assets and not get laid every night?

How is that even the same? Katie didn't like this turn in the conversation. She wished Pandora would refocus on Batman.

Trust me, it is. Besides, Bane isn't really a villain, not like the Joker or the Riddler. He's just a guy who helped a little girl and said, 'Fuck the system.' Then, he did everything he could to make sure she carried out her father's legacy. I mean, he was just doing what he promised. The others were senseless and crazy. Don't get me wrong, I love senseless and crazy, but Bane is like a furry kitten compared to them.

Katie shook her head, awestruck by Pandora's logic. *What? He is helping her blow up Gotham City with a nuclear weapon because* why? *She has daddy issues? Fuck, we all have daddy issues, but you don't see me trying to blow up a city over it. Get laid again, but this time enjoy it, ferchrissakes.*

Like you have room to talk.

Katie narrowed her brow. *I got* laid, *remember?*

Pandora scoffed. *I didn't realize that you only needed it like once every ten years.*

I wanted to make sure I wasn't a deadly lay first.

That would be a hell of a superhero movie. You'd be like Poison Ivy, except a kiss of the Vagina would do a guy in instead of the lipstick. You could just go around banging all the hot bad guys. You get laid and do a public service. It's two birds with one vagina.

Katie rolled her eyes. *Except it would have to be the finale that killed them. Otherwise, it would be a life of missed orgasms, and that might turn me into a true villain.*

Too true, but I'm sure we could get Batman a rubber dick for his suit. Then you could go to town, and no one would die.

Katie swung her feet off the bed and rubbed her eye with the heel of her hand. *I don't even know how I get into these conversations. I need coffee and breakfast.*

It was at that moment that Katie realized it had already been two days since Pandora had asked for any type of donut, but she wasn't about to say a word.

Katie yawned as she walked out of her bedroom. She shuffled down the hallway, smelling the sweet scent of coffee and bacon coming from the kitchen. When she rounded the corner, there was Angie, standing right inside the door and holding out a mug of hot coffee to her.

Katie pulled the mug to her face, taking a deep whiff and smiling. "You are my savior."

Angie chuckled. "Don't let the angel hear that."

Katie furrowed her brow and looked at Angie over the rim of the cup. "Hey, I do what I want."

Angie gave her a crooked smile. "Okay. Well, if you *want*, come sit with me at the kitchen table and have some bacon and eggs. I just finished cooking."

Katie raised her eyebrows and smiled as she sauntered over to the table and sat down. "Don't mind if I do."

They sat there for a moment, quietly enjoying their breakfasts and coffees. The sun was starting to shine in through the large windows, casting rays of light across the condo. Angie took a bite of her eggs and glanced at the park, then leaned forward to look down at the sidewalk.

She sighed and shook her head, sitting back and looking at Katie. She didn't want to tell her, but she also didn't want to let her walk out of the building without being aware. Angie fiddled with the food on her plate for a moment and then brought it up carefully. "So, there are a bunch of people on the sidewalk outside the front doors."

Without thinking, Katie blurted, "For what?"

Angie's shoulders went up, and she grimaced. "To meet you."

"Oh, God. Are they perverts?"

Pandora laughed snidely. *If they are, maybe I'll see some action. My luck, though, they will be a bunch of angel worshipers coming to lay hands on you...and not in a good way.*

Angie peeked at the people below again. "Well, I can't say that *none* of them are pervs, but most of them seem to be acting like they are waiting for a rock star or something."

Instantly, Pandora was filled with excitement. *Hell, yeah. We have fans now, which means you need to look your best when we walk out of here. Don't embarrass me. There may be some fantastic pictures taken.*

Katie saw the opportunity immediately. "Or maybe they think I'm an apostle."

Oh, hell no.

Angie giggled, knowing they were messing with Pandora. "Or a holy woman."

Pandora started laughing loudly, not even able to form the words. She giggled and snorted for several moments until something popped into her head, then shut up real fast and huffed. *As chaste as you are, you are probably more holy than most holy men. Probably. Well, maybe not. But I would have to say you're more chaste than many of them, especially with all the drama going on in the church. Talk about perverts!*

Can we not ruin my breakfast with a conversation about pedophilia?

Pandora became indignant. *Hey, your friend brought it up.*

Katie leaned over and looked down at the group of people on the sidewalk. She took a sip of her coffee and exhaled, letting her breath fog the window and obscure the crowd. Pandora might think it was awesome that she was so famous, but Katie thought it was inconvenient. "Great. *Now* how am I supposed to leave?"

They sat quietly for a moment, then Angie shrugged and pointed at the ceiling. Katie looked up, and quickly caught on to what she was suggesting.

She leaned her head back in defeat. "Dammit, that wasn't what I had in mind when all this happened. I did not plan on jumping from building to building like freaking Spiderman."

Angie gave her a comforting look. "It could be worse. You could be Affleck."

Pandora perked up. *Wait, what was that about leaping from building to building?*

Katie let out a deep sigh and shrugged her shoulders. "Fuck it. I wanted to work with the general anyway."

Stop. Who's Spiderman? What are you talking about?

Katie took the last bite of her bacon and headed toward her bedroom. She grabbed her normal guns and put them in the holsters at her sides. She ran her hands over Tom and Harry, but they were too big to take just anywhere.

Pandora cleared her throat and nonchalantly pointed out, *You should take your jacket.*

Why? It's warm outside.

Yeah, but you'll look great in it.

Katie frowned, thinking about how warm it would be and how out of place she would look. *No, I'll look like I can't figure out how hot it is.*

Pandora let out a squeak of excitement. *You know what we need? We need a cape.*

No. Not only no, but hell *no. What happens when the cape gets grabbed? It's bad for fighting, which ultimately leads to being bad for keeping me alive.*

But bad for fighting or not, it would look fucking sweet.

Katie rolled her eyes and shook her head, then arranged the last of her weapons and switched off her bedroom light. *Tight leather with carbon-fiber bullet protection is going to have to do for now.*

You are no fun. We could make the damn cape black, like your soul.

Katie laughed. *According to Gabriel, my soul isn't all black.*

Pandora silently sneered. *Yeah, you've got some unicorn-glitter shit going on inside you too, but I don't hold that against you.*

I appreciate it.

Angie walked out of the kitchen, wiping her hands on a towel. "Got a job?"

Katie smiled and grabbed the keys, hanging them on her belt loop. "No, I have a meeting, but I can't say when, where, or with whom."

Angie gave her side-eye. "Okay?"

Katie went for the door, already running late. "I'll tell you later. I should be back soon, but you know how to get me."

Angie nodded and waved as Katie left. "The demon signal—got it." Angie heard Katie snarl from the hallway and grinned as she went back to the kitchen.

Normally, Katie would take the elevator down to the bottom floor, but this time she knew that going out the front door was a bad idea. When she reached the elevators, she turned right instead and took the stairs all the way to the top. She lifted her key ring and grabbed the card key on the end, sliding it into the security lock.

How did you get that?

Security. They shared it with me just in case I had to get out of the building another way. Katie dropped the keyring and kicked open the door dramatically.

Oh? And why exactly are you using it now?

Katie shrugged and tugged on her belt, making sure it was firmly in place. *Because I don't know who's down there or what they want, and I'm not going to get into a fight in the middle of the street.*

Yeah, but why are you up here? *Oh, shit. Wait, wait,* wait*! I thought we were going to talk about thisssssss...*

Katie sprinted across the roof, then took one large step onto the edge and leaped off the building. She flew through the air for a brief, terrifying moment before her wings popped open and spread wide, then caught an updraft. Her wings carried her over the tops of the buildings and down three blocks. Katie could feel Pandora clenching inside her, but she ignored the demon. Instead, Katie circled and took in the view around them, relishing the feel of the wind on her face, and enjoying the freedom of soaring through the sky.

When she neared her destination, she flapped her wings and slowed her momentum. She hovered over the open-air rooftop café and slowly descended. She barely skipped when she stepped onto the deck, and she collapsed her wings effortlessly. She was proud of how good she was getting at sticking her landings.

Both customers and servers were shocked to see her, and Katie waved to a few patrons. As she wove through the tables and over to the elevators she heard them whispering, but no one said anything to her. She pressed the call button, and as she waited, she straightened her top and flattened her windswept hair. She still found it amusing when people looked at her with open mouths and wide eyes. No matter how many times she saw their reactions, it didn't get old.

Pandora finally caught her breath. *Fuck it. You're a demon-fucking-angel. Let them stare.*

For several moments, the restaurant was silent, and Katie stood whistling to herself, feeling a dozen pairs of eyes boring into the back of her head. Let them stare. Finally, the doors opened with a ding, and she stepped inside. She pressed the bottom floor button and waited to turn around until she heard the doors close.

Katie fidgeted in irritation. *Demon-fucking-angel or not, I hate it when they stare.*

Maybe you shouldn't drop into a rooftop restaurant, then. Just a thought.

The doors opened on the first floor, and Katie hurried out of the building and onto the sidewalk, then got her bearings and made her way to the meeting spot that the general had texted her. There were a ton of people on the street, but none of them seemed to notice her—or if they did, they didn't care. That was one thing she loved about New York City. Most of the time no one paid any attention, even to people dressed like her.

Katie hurried down the street and around the corner to a parking lot. There was an SUV parked there, its windows tinted jet-black.

Katie swaggered forward, crossing her arms. *How obvious is that?*

As she approached the SUV, she stopped in her tracks and watched as a blonde woman with a three-year-old girl stepped out of the vehicle onto the sidewalk. Katie looked at them for a moment, thinking that she might have been wrong, and the sound of a horn honking behind her made her jump. She spun to see the general's bushy eyebrows through the front windshield of a beat-up sedan that had been old a decade ago.

Katie tilted her head, confused, but hurried over to the car and climbed inside. She closed the door and glared at the general, who was quietly laughing at her. It was obvious she had made the assumption that stealth or not, he would arrive in a blacked-out SUV.

The general got hold of himself, tamping down the amusement as best he could. "I told you I wanted to be nondescript. A government SUV on the corner of a New York City street isn't necessarily what I would call being in disguise."

Katie shook her head. "I know, but I just figured… Fuck it."

The general took off down the street, still chuckling. He drove for a few blocks and turned into an alley in a quiet part of the town. He gestured for Katie to follow, and the two got out of the car and walked two more blocks. He led her into a large parking garage.

As they rounded the corner on the fourth floor, Katie sniggered. The only car on this level was a giant blacked-out SUV. "Hey, I got it half right."

The general opened the door for Katie, and they both climbed into the back. The general waved at the driver, and they left the parking garage and drove around town. Brushwood let out a deep sigh and took off his hat, putting it on his lap and looking at Katie. "You look well. I had concerns after that fight in England."

Katie pursed her lips and did her best to answer nonchalantly. "It wasn't as clean as I'd have liked it to be, but the job got done."

"That it did. Because of our efforts there, they are now in talks with your weaponry company." The general made quotation marks with his fingers before continuing, "They will be a force to be reckoned with when they are all trained. We're sending some of our guys over there as consultants to whip them into shape."

"Good. I want them to be just as prepared as we are," Katie urged passionately. "This isn't a fight for the United States. This is a worldwide battle. Every single life on the planet is at stake."

The general didn't say a word, just stared out the window as they pulled into an old airfield on the outskirts of town. "You're right, and I like that you think that way."

The SUV came to a stop, and Katie peeked out the window and smiled when she saw a fat tan military helicopter with its rotors spinning. They got out of the vehicle and Katie followed the general, bending low and walking across the helo pad with her hair whipping crazily in the wind. The general helped her in, then nodded at the pilot and put his headphones on, ready to start the conversation.

5

Angie hurried through the precinct and across the main room to the conference area. The chief and several others were waiting for her there. She had to check in on their efforts. Timothy wouldn't be there in person, but he was on the line, conferenced in to hear all about it. When she entered, they were all sitting around the table eating donuts and laughing. They quieted down and straightened up when they saw her.

Angie stood at the head of the table. "I know you guys are busy, so I will keep this as short as possible. I wanted an update, then I'll let you get back to it."

The chief stood up and looked around. "We all have to agree, it's going ten times better than we thought it would. It pains my precinct budget to say so, but if things continue in this manner, it will be worth every penny. Not to mention the countless lives it will save, and already *has* saved."

Timothy's voice emerged from the speaker of Angie's phone. "That's what *I'm* talkin' about."

Angie cleared her throat. "You're on speaker, Timothy."

"Oh, uh, I mean, I'm glad you are pleased," he corrected in the most professional voice he could muster.

Angie took the phone off speaker and held it up to her ear. "Do you have any questions?"

Timothy cleared his throat, embarrassed. "No, I just wanted to hear that it was all going well. If they have any questions, just call me back. I've never been good on conference calls."

Angie chuckled. "You could have fooled me."

Angie pressed End and shook her head, then collected herself and peered at the officers, who had begun talking amongst themselves. "Do you guys have any questions?"

An officer with a thin mustache cleared his throat and stuck up his hand. "Yes, but it's not really about the system."

Angie sighed. What now? "Okay, shoot."

He looked at the man next to him, who nodded and prodded him with an elbow. "How's Katie?"

Angie grinned and picked up her purse. "She's good. Apparently, Pandora is starting to want to play Batman."

Two of the cops looked quickly at each other, concerned. "Oh, shit."

They quickly huddled together and Angie narrowed her eyes, watching them as they whispered to one another. The cop with the mustache shook his head and left the room, and she turned from the closing door to face the remaining officers. Angie didn't know what was going on. Whatever it was, it had worried both of them—and she knew it had something to do with Katie and Pandora.

Angie raised her eyebrow and tilted her head. "Was it something I said?"

The chief shook his head, taking a sip of his coffee. "No, not at all. It's okay, just dealing with a potential oops before it becomes real."

"I thought you were going to bring lunch?" The general grinned at her.

Katie nodded and smirked. "I should've picked it up on the way here. Unfortunately, I've had to deal with Wonder Woman in my psyche."

"I'm not exactly sure what you're referring to, but I never imagined Pandora as Wonder Woman."

For God sakes, woman, you're talking in riddles. Let me handle this. Pandora took over Katie's speech. "What's up, Papa Brushwood? Yeah, it's Pandora. I took over."

The general coughed and sat up straighter. "Hello, Pandora."

Pandora clicked her tongue and pulled Katie's hands over her face, giving her a mask of fingers. She lowered her voice to a growl. "So here's the thing… Katie and Angie showed me *Batman,* and I'm pretty pissed that's been kept from me this whole time."

The general narrowed his eyes. "Batman?"

Pandora continued in her normal voice, "Not Batman exactly, but the fact that there are actual superheroes. Vigilantes who are out there, saving people's lives and even working with the government like we do. She made it seem like what we do is wild and crazy. The truth is, they've actually made movies about it. Superheroes are pretty much the shit! It seems I'm the only one who sees this similarity."

The general tilted his head to the side. "So, am I to understand you find superhero movies interesting? I enjoy superhero movies just like the rest of them, I'll admit. I wouldn't think the vigilante aspect would spark your interest, though. My guess is you're more interested in the villains."

Pandora gasped. "I'm not the villain, am I? Besides, it's a bunch of hot men in tight suits bending over and showing off their assets. They beat people up and destroy shit. Couldn't ask for better television."

The general laughed loudly and shook his head. "I guess you're right. I do enjoy it when they blow up shit in movies. I used to think that didn't actually happen in real life—until I met the two of you, that is. It seems like wherever you two are, something's falling down."

Pandora bared her teeth. "Yeah, but it's falling into a pile of demon dust. That's why we're here in the first place. We don't really blow shit up, though. Not very often, at least. It's usually more of a crumbling building than a car bursting into flames. I mean, we can change that if you want. I'd have to get with Timothy about some new ordnance."

Pandora put her hands over her eyes and made her voice a growl again. "You could be my commissioner." She had the next *Batman* all planned out in her head.

The general shook his head. "No, I think I'm good with my current job. And it's hard enough for me to explain the amount of destruction you cause as it is. I'm just lucky that it's usually because of some horrifying demon who ends up dead, and that it leads directly to hundreds, if not thousands, of lives being saved. If it weren't for that, I'm not sure how I could keep you guys on the books."

"You could make a movie about us. You wouldn't even have to re-shoot. You could just have a cameraman follow us around everywhere."

The general humored her with a smile. "I could, but I think I would probably need a whole *fleet* of cameramen to follow you around. The fatality rate of those who work beside you isn't exactly low."

Pandora pointed her finger at the general. "Good thought. We would definitely need at least a dozen."

The general looked up as the pilot moved the helicopter higher. When they reached five thousand feet, the pilot gave the general a nod. Brushwood nodded back and sat up straight, turning toward Katie. "Okay, we're here. What did you want to talk about or show me?"

Pandora was still in control, and she shrugged. "Beats the fuck out of me. I'm just the passenger."

The general was genuinely surprised and slightly suspicious. "*What?* I thought you knew everything that Katie knew, and the other way around. At least, it seems that way most of the time."

"Yeah, well, it's not like she asks my permission or anything. She just pokes and prods around. She gets a few special appendages, and then *WHAM*—big head syndrome commences." Pandora lifted her hands and mimed her words, puffing Katie's cheeks out and rolling her eyes.

The general covered his mouth and laughed, trying to hide his amusement at Pandora's sarcasm. "I guess we all need to keep secrets now and then, even those of us with someone else in our head. Not that I would know how that feels. I've managed to stay demon-free."

"What is it that you humans say? Oh, 'knock on wood' on that one. Don't want to go jinxing yourself or anything."

The general ran his eyes over the interior of the helicopter and knocked on the window. "That will have to do. As much as I appreciate you and Katie and our relationship, I'm pretty sure I wouldn't be that lucky."

Pandora locked her hands behind Katie's head. "Not very many people can be this lucky. Not only am I a savage hellfire-raised warrior queen of a demon, but I'm here to help you humans keep your heads on your shoulders. The rest of them end up with idiot demons who don't even know what they're doing."

"So I've seen."

Suddenly, Katie's arms flew down to her sides, and her eyes shut tightly. Her shoulders went limp and then her eyes slowly opened again, a red sparkle in her pupils. She rubbed her face, groaning with irritation. "*Wow*, she has a big mouth."

The general raised his eyebrows but didn't say a word. Katie stretched her arms over her head and cracked her neck, then leaned forward and tapped the pilot on the shoulder, lifting one side of his headset off his ear. "What are we, about five thousand feet up?"

The pilot gave Katie a thumbs-up, and she patted him on the shoulder. "Good. Hover here."

She leaned back in her chair and smiled sweetly at the general, straightening her holsters and stretching her arms.

He looked at her, amused but confused. She leaned over. "Got everything you need?"

The general narrowed his eyes. "What?" She was already up and reaching for the door handle, and his eyes popped wide open as she slid the door open and air rushed into the passenger compartment. When he finally realized what she was about to do he tried to back up.

Katie reached over and undid his seatbelt. She waved her hand at the open door and yelled over the roar of the helicopter's engine, "C'mon!"

He shook his head feverishly, pointing to his back. "No way. No parachute, and we're way too low anyway!"

Katie shrugged. "I don't need one!"

"Yeah, but what about me?"

Katie sighed, then grabbed the general by his arms and leaped backward out the door. The general froze in her arms as they plummeted earthward. Katie waited an extra half a second and then her wings sprouted, caught air, and jerked them upward. She twisted the general around and hugged him tightly. Her wings beat heavily and carried them away from the roar of the helicopter.

The general looked around wildly, then gulped in air and tried to calm himself. "I didn't realize you could carry two so easily."

Katie giggled. "Neither did I. I just had faith that I wasn't given secondhand wings."

The general resisted the urge to panic and flail. He was in the arms of a mercenary who had wings, flying thousands of feet above the middle of nowhere. Instead of panicking, he slowed his breathing. He peered carefully at

Katie's face and decided that he could trust her. They had been through too much together for him not to.

He figured she wouldn't fly him out to the middle of nowhere just to drop him five thousand feet to the ground, so he took another deep breath and studied his surroundings. Now that he was calm, he could appreciate just how beautiful it was that high up. He had never had a view quite like that, out in the open air without a helicopter around him. He had a feeling he would never have a view like it again.

Hell, even if he *did* die, it was a good way to go.

Katie pumped her wings as she watched the general relax and begin to take in the view. After all, it was pretty amazing from up there. *She* rarely took the time to enjoy it. She should learn to sit back and take in the moment, even if it was just for a second.

Deep beneath the ocean's surface, the dark current flowed quietly and strongly, feeding the ecosystem beneath the waves. Schools of fish swam freely through the water near the surface, shifting and moving as larger fish moved in and out, looking for their next meal.

From a thin crack in the seafloor, a plume of bubbles began to trickle, then the trickle became a stream. Bubbles shot up through the current and scattered the schools of fish.

The seafloor rumbled with seismic activity. Sand and coral dislodged as the ground shook, sending grit up to cloud the water. A small mountain began to shift slowly, and the mud and rocks around it on the seafloor broke loose. Long-trapped air rushed in every direction, and streams of bubbles and sediment sent the schools of fish swimming in a hundred different directions.

The earthquake increased in intensity, and rocks and sediment swirled along the seafloor. The underwater mountain broke loose and drifted upward, creating waves when it surfaced. It bobbed in the waves like some massive, impossible buoy.

Huge chunks of mud and rock began to fall off the mountain, revealing dark, slick scales.

This was no mountain. The echo of a groan rose from deep under the ocean, and then something broke the surface and stretched high into the air. The last of the rocks broke free as it fully extended. It wasn't some ancient shard of the Earth's crust, but a giant arm. Enormous and scaled, it dripped seawater and the corpses of a hundred fish.

The sea had been hiding a secret, too far out for any sailors to see, but too close to land for it not to be a complete and total disaster waiting to happen.

The ocean raged. The seafloor shook. And danger slowly made its way out of the depths toward land.

6

Katie looked behind her to make sure the helicopter was maintaining a safe distance. The pilot was protecting the general, but he had made sure to wave the craft off as soon as he realized he was safe. He didn't need him shooting down his only ally, or at least his only ally with a chance of fighting the Damned.

Katie looked around her for any sign of spies but saw only open fields below and clear sky above. "I just wanted to make sure it was safe to talk. I know that you are worried about the conversation being bugged. This was all that I could think of, so hopefully we're safe here."

The general glanced from side to side. "Who the hell is going to bug the air around us, even if they could?"

"That's exactly what I was thinking."

The general let out a bellowing laugh and nodded. "I suppose you're right. It was the possibility of being bugged that was worrying me."

"I don't know why you're so concerned with that. The

demons don't use bugs, and the rest of them? I don't waste time thinking about them."

The general looked at her intently. "Katie, you have to understand something. *Everyone* wants you right now. The government wants you to play Captain America for hearts and minds."

Pandora was almost offended by the thought. *Captain America is a pussy. From what I found out last night, he cheated his way into the system to be a superhero.*

Katie ignored Pandora and tried to focus on the general. He was serious about what he was saying, but in a way she recognized as caring. "There are those in the government who want to dissect you to figure out if they can use you or duplicate you to make an army. Some of them want you to come to Washington to protect their important asses."

Pandora scoffed. *Oh, that's rich, since half of them are Damned. They are just trying to trick the system. There's no way they would want you actually around.*

The general sighed and shrugged his shoulders. "Then there are the churches. Many of the religious people want you."

Pandora cackled loudly. *That's it! That is the answer. You could deflower the hierarchy of the church and bring it down with just a few strokes.*

Lord, please don't continue. I'm actually trying to have a conversation here, Pandora. I know you're a demon, but if you could hold back on the church comments for just a few minutes, maybe I could get something accomplished.

Pandora was off in her own little conniving world at that point. *Yeah... I'm thinking you start at the bottom and work your way up to the Pope. By the time you're done, you'll be wearing the hat, standing on the balcony, and waving at the believers.*

Katie chuckled and wrinkled her nose. *I have never looked good in hats.*

Then you can wear the robes and nothing else. It'll be a new day for the Catholic Church.

My grandmother is rolling over in her grave right now. Seriously, if there's an afterlife, I'd rather burn in hell than face Grandma after this conversation.

Meh, you'll be fine.

The general continued talking, not realizing Katie was having a conversation with Pandora in her head. "Then there are those who feel you're going to become a danger to society."

Katie looked down, surprised at the general. "Why?"

"Because you're going to become a symbol. I mean, you already fly and kill demons when others can't, and let's face it—you aren't unattractive."

Katie scowled and gritted her teeth, making a face like an angry child. "That's Pandora!"

"Who is also you, if you haven't looked in the mirror lately."

Katie shook her head. "I don't want this, General."

"Doesn't matter what you want. You can't command what others think, and if you could, it would just prove their point. You are officially the most powerful person in this country. The expectation is that you will become the most powerful person in the world in the next five years, give or take a few elected officials and the occasional despot."

"Don't forget work. I could be dead next week."

The general grumped. "That would cause those people's worries to go away."

Katie rolled her eyes and sighed. "Not how I expected you to react."

"What? You didn't think I became a general without keeping my sense of humor, did you?"

Katie flapped her wings a couple of times and stared at the mountains in the far distance. "I want them to know that I'm not trying to take over or use my power to rule the world or anything like that. I'm using it to save lives."

"Welcome to politics, where no good deed goes unpunished. If you're more powerful than someone else, they try to act like your friend while they secretly make plans to stab you in the back. These people are afraid that the masses will follow you and leave all government behind."

Katie shook her head and wrinkled her face in anger. "That's ridiculous. I'm just one person, and I'm no saint. I don't hide that."

"Which makes you even more relatable. I'm not saying you should change who you are. What I'm saying is, you have to be careful. The more powers you have and the more people you save, the more people will come after you. Sure, some are just curious, but most of them want to control you in some way, shape, or form. And if they can't do that, they're going to want to be close to you so that when you reach power, or when *they* think you reach power, they will be right there beside you and not stuck back with everyone else."

Katie sighed and lowered her head. "Sometimes I think maybe I should just let the demons take us all. Don't get me wrong, there's a bunch of beauty in this world. Its safety has fallen into my hands, and I take that seriously. But sometimes it's really difficult to remember why I fight so hard to save it."

The general returned her sigh, but with a sense of hope hidden beneath. "I know. Do you remember that fight where I picked up that little girl and ran full speed across the field full of demons?"

Katie shifted the general in her arms, realizing they were getting tired. "Yeah, that was pretty much one of the coolest things I've ever seen!"

"Well, remember her face? You need to. You need to remember that her mother was infected. *That's* why we want to save humanity."

Katie nodded. "I suppose. Do you really think that nothing in my life is safe? I mean, are they listening to me and watching me at all times?"

"I don't know the whens or the wheres, but yes, I think we're all being bugged. When we get back to Earth, I'll give you some contacts, and they can help you clean up the bugs. You need a professional."

Katie shook her head. "I've got my own professional. I need to have somebody I trust do it. It's not going to do much good if I send someone in to debug me, and they're the ones that end up actually bugging me. I'll just need to know that you think you're clean, too. And if you don't trust your people, let me know when I can send my person."

"Of course. There's a private guy I completely and totally trust to do the service for me, but I'll let you know if anything happens to him. I think you are best utilized doing what you do where you're free to do it however you want. It's hard enough being you, I'm sure. On top of that, you have to worry about what everybody thinks and feels, and who's safe or not. Now you have to worry about people coming after you and listening to every single one of your conversations. I'm sure it's not easy to just relax and let it go."

Katie narrowed her eyes and gazed at the horizon, taking a deep breath and letting it out slowly. She had been fighting all of it, and she hadn't even realized that she had been doing it until that moment. Outwardly, she looked like she was herself, but in reality, she was holding everything back. She was too worried about what other people would think, not realizing it was taking a huge toll on her. "General, I think I'm going to need to own who I am and revel in it to get some of these people to back down."

He sighed. "I have no idea what that means."

"I don't have a damned clue, either, but I know who to ask if he would just show up. It's not easy for me to ask for his help, and Pandora doesn't make it any easier."

Katie could almost feel Pandora grow indignant as she shouted, *Damn right, I'm not going to make it easy. You think he's angelic, but that's just because you have an English definition of the word. You haven't seen what I've seen.*

Maybe not, but I do know he's the only one that can help us right now. You're just gonna have to suck it up.

Pandora was silent, and Katie was thankful. She didn't want to argue with her about Gabriel anymore. She glanced at the horizon one last time and then at the ground, finding a large open field where the helicopter could land to pick up the general. Slowly and carefully, she descended, and she bent her legs as her feet touched the grass.

She set the general down. To his credit, he only stumbled momentarily. He cleared his throat, straightened his tie, and pulled down his jacket, then stood up straight and proud. Katie thought he looked like he had spent the afternoon in a boardroom, rather than flying thousands of feet though in the open air in her clutches. He regarded her seriously. "I've never regretted believing in you, Katie."

Katie studied him for a moment, only having felt the pull of a father figure once before in her life. It touched her, and she felt the emotion more strongly than she had ever thought she would. She reached up and wiped a single tear away from her cheek. She saw him watching, so she chuckled nervously and shook her head. "General, you're one of the few men I respect who isn't on my team. I want you to know that I'll always have your back."

The general inclined his head slightly and patted her on the back, then performed a crisp about-face and headed toward the landing chopper. Katie stood there as the general climbed aboard, and he turned and waved at her. He favored her with one last smile before shutting the door behind him. Katie covered her eyes and tilted her head down as the helo took off. It climbed briefly and then sped off into the distance.

She breathed deeply, shaking her head as she turned to look around her.

Pandora groaned. *Well, this is just fucking great. Now we're in the middle of a fucking field with not a taxi in sight, and there goes our ride.*

Katie took in her surroundings, ignoring Pandora's irritation. She knew she was all alone in the field and that they would have to make it back to the city, but her mind was on something completely different. She was no longer worried about things like that. She was going to force herself to start being the person that she knew she was.

Katie felt her shoulders raise and her spirits with them. *I'm done acting like I'm the same as everyone else.*

Look, I've told you for a while now that you gotta be you. Wait, what are you gonna do?

Switch with me. Take over my body, but let me be in your head.

Pandora readied herself slowly, unsure where this was going. *Okay.*

Katie held the air in her lungs and closed her eyes, feeling the heat of Pandora's soul taking over her body. When she opened her eyes again, she could see what Pandora was seeing, but she was on the inside. For the first time in a while, she felt like she could actually relax.

Okay. We're going to work on you bringing out our wings and putting them back. Katie had opened herself up and was ready for it.

I'm not exactly sure what I'm doing, but I'll give it my best shot.

Pandora centered herself and closed her eyes, imagining the wings on her back. Katie did the same, helping her along until the wings appeared. Pandora opened her eyes and looked back, flapping them strongly and laughing. "Well, *this* is damn cool. Hold on, let me try to put them back and bring them back out again."

Pandora concentrated hard and felt the tingle across her back as the wings folded in and then disappeared. She took a deep breath and popped them back out, smiling and clapping her hands as they flapped wildly behind her. Katie grinned at Pandora's response, finding it humorous that suddenly she was so engrossed with the wings when she had hated them just a week before.

Katie looked around through Pandora's vision, seeing the edges of the wings flapping behind her. *Okay, I want you to try to pull them out while I'm fighting you.*

Pandora put the wings away and closed her eyes, concentrating hard on pulling the wings out. Katie was concentrating harder, though. She did not want the wings to come out, and it was working. No matter how hard Pandora tried, the wings stayed inside.

Katie panted, letting go of her concentration. *So, we know now that you can't use the wings without my permission.*

Oh, great—just what I need. Something else for you to control.

Katie ignored her. She knew Pandora was going to enjoy what she had in store. *Since the helicopter's gone and we're in the middle of nowhere, why don't you give these wings a try?*

Hell, *yeah!*

Now, your first time, you want to take it easy. Otherwise, you're going to end up hurting yourself, and more importantly, me.

Pfft, I got this.

Katie sighed and let her have her way. She watched as Pandora took off across the field, flapping her wings. Her feet gently lifted off the ground, then settled back down. Pandora huffed and puffed, pumping her arms as she ran and straining her wings to try to get herself into the air.

When she reached her top speed, she leaped and flapped even harder. She lifted for a brief, beautiful moment, then wobbled, and in another heartbeat, she fell back down.

She grunted as she landed face-first in a mud puddle.

Katie snickered. *You want some donuts?*

Pandora exulted. *Girl, I was playing word games to win since before your eldest grandmother knew what her fun box was for. I'm not eating a donut no matter how much you tempt me.*

Are you sure? All I can think about is when the Krispy Kreme donuts come out fresh, hot, and ready, with their slightly crispy outer shell and soft, airy insides. The glaze just drips off your fingers, and you can lick it right up. Oh! And I forgot to tell you, I heard that it's Krispy Kreme's anniversary, and if you buy a dozen donuts, you get the second dozen for just a dollar. That's double the delicious, sweet perfection for half the price.

Pandora gritted her teeth and shook her head, then pulled herself to her feet and set off at a run. She worked her wings furiously, and cut her eyes at Katie.

"You know, you can be a real bitch sometimes."

7

"You called for me?" Moloch grumbled as he stepped out of the portal. He looked down at the humans and flexed his large, hideous muscles.

The two mercenary contacts that Moloch had been using to find the whereabouts of the weapons factory stood there shuddering in their shoes. They may be on his side, but they were absolutely terrified of him.

One of the two stepped forward and nodded. "We… have some GPS coordinates for you to help you find the base."

Moloch growled, annoyed by this. "What demon uses GPS?"

"Well, you can use them on more than just a GPS. You can find them on Google maps or whatever it is that you use to locate people," the other mercenary sputtered.

Moloch narrowed his eyes, not believing that he had found two people so stupid as to think that demons actually used human coordinates to find things. If that were the case, he could have easily done this legwork himself. He didn't walk around glued to a cell phone like so many of the meatsacks he came upon. He found little use for technology unless it had to do with destroying humanity or bringing more souls to hell.

Moloch showed the men his teeth. "I don't use any of that. Have I been mistaken? Are you two idiots that stupid? If you are, I can promise you it's not going to go over well with me. I can always use a couple of new souls in hell, but I try to make sure they're at least somewhat intelligent."

One of the men gulped and pulled out his cell phone. He held it to Moloch with a shaking hand. "It's an Android, I don't like it anyway."

Moloch took the phone from him and stared at the thing with confusion. He was not even sure his large fingers could press the buttons.

The other guy stepped to Moloch and carefully reached over the demon's arm. He turned the phone on. Moloch breathed foul breath on him, but let the man work the device. He pulled up the map and entered the coordinates. "See, if you put in the coordinates here, it'll show you exactly where you need to go. If you press maps, it will give you step-by-step directions how to get there from exactly where you are—though I'm assuming you are not going to be traveling by car."

Moloch growled again and shoved the phone back at the man. "No, you would be correct. I don't drive around all over creation looking for weapons manufacturers. That was supposed to be your job!"

Moloch stood up to his full height. He scratched his craggy chin with his scaled hand, annoyed with the technology and annoyed with the men that were standing in front of him. After some thought, he reached out and grabbed both men by throats. "Keep your phone. I'll take your souls."

Both men yelled loudly as a portal ripped open behind them. Moloch roared laughter and pushed them through the opening, all the way down to hell. The demon landed, still clutching the men by their throats. He took in the look on their terrified faces.

"Tell me, where does your GPS say you are now?"

Katie looked out the window at swarms of people on the New York City street below. She was happy to be home. Her trip back to the city wasn't all that bad, especially since Pandora was learning to fly. She definitely worked up an appetite. As soon as they got back to the city, they went straight to Little Italy to get their favorite foods.

Okay, I'll agree on starting out with just the ravioli and the cheese bread appetizer, but that doesn't mean I agree to stop there.

Katie chuckled. *I'm not going to argue with you. You worked pretty hard out there, and you deserve a little reward— though I would appreciate it if every time we dropped back down you didn't scream, "I am Batman."*

Hey, until I get my own line, I'm using that one, but I guess I could tone it down just a bit. I'm pretty sure I scared the shit out of that farmer when I clipped his hat with your wings.

Katie smirked, trying not to let anyone see she was having a conversation in her head. *Yeah, I would say you did. The poor man is never going to be the same.*

Meh, he'll just think he was abducted by aliens or something like that. No biggie.

At least it will make for a fucking hilarious news report.

The front door of the restaurant opened, and Detective Schultz and Detective Travers ambled in. They stopped at the hostess stand and spoke to the hostess quietly. She glanced nervously at Katie and then pointed the two detectives in her direction.

Pandora was a little peeved. *You would think that if they saw a girl eating at a table, they would give her a chance to finish the damn meal. I mean, seriously! When they get over here, don't you stop eating.*

The detectives stared across the dining room and smiled at Katie. She ignored them and took a huge bite of her ravioli.

Okay. But I've always been told it's rude to talk with your mouthful.

Hey, they walked into one of the exceptions. They have no idea just how many calories flying takes. I'm not even going to have to reroute these calories until we get to the third course.

Katie swallowed hard, shaking her head. *Whoa, whoa, whoa. Who said anything about a third course?*

I told you I wasn't done at ravioli.

Yeah, but I thought you meant like maybe another couple slices of garlic bread and some tiramisu. I didn't think that you are gonna go all out, like that first time we went to the Italian restaurant in Las Vegas.

Pandora snorted laughter. *Oh, that was priceless. That next morning when Damien knocked on the door, you scared the crap out of him. I think I replayed his face in my mind at least a hundred times. He wasn't sure whether you were having an orgasm or your appendix had burst. Either way, he looked like he was about to fall to pieces.*

Katie coughed, then got ahold of herself and finished swallowing another bite of ravioli. *I almost forgot about that. I was so miserable I thought I would never feel better.*

And there you were. Just a young girl not even realizing your tits were growing bigger and your waist was growing smaller. It's all in the magic, my friend, all in the magic.

The detectives stopped a few feet away, whispering to one another.

Well, apparently now all I have to do is stretch my wings.

Pandora winced, making a hissing sound. *We are going to keep a tight lock on how much you go flying. I can't keep you in this luscious figure with too much of it, you burn way too many calories. You'll become all stringy, like that old yoga woman on TV.*

I'll file that away for later.

Travers and Schultz arrived at the table. They waited to be acknowledged. When they were not, Travers pointed to the seat next to Katie. "You mind if we take a seat?"

Katie swallowed a bite of food. "By all means."

Travers pulled out the chair and sat down. "Sorry to bother you while you're eating. We've been trying to hunt you down for a couple of days now. We know you're busy, this won't take long."

Schultz waved the waitress away as she walked up. She spun on her heels and walked away. He leaned toward Katie. "How have you been?"

Katie wiped her mouth with her napkin and set it on the table. "Good. You know, the usual. I'm always on the watch for the demons. How about you guys, how have you been? How are your families?"

Travers nodded and cleared his throat. "Good. They're seeing more of us these days."

Schultz nodded his head in agreement. "My wife is definitely enjoying the time with me, that's for sure."

Katie stared at them slightly confused. "But the precinct has been so busy. Where's all this free time coming from?"

Travers sat back and gestured for Schultz to take the lead. "We haven't been working too hard these last few weeks. The system you have definitely works, but the calls aren't even close to being as frequent as they once were."

Schultz helped himself to a piece of garlic bread.

Pandora growled. *Slap his hand!*

"I think the demons know you're in town, so they're keeping their heads down. Not that I blame them. You are definitely one tough son of a bitch, excuse the language."

Katie grabbed the last piece of garlic bread before Travers could claim it. "Please, you've heard my mouth. I can't even explain to you what Pandora's is like."

Both the detectives grinned and shifted their eyes to their hands. "Fair enough. But I was taught not to cuss around the ladies."

Pandora scoffed. *You have them really confused and fooled.*

Katie feigned confusion. "Apparently no one taught me proper etiquette."

Travers smiled and shook his head. "But see, it's all part of your charm. I would think something was wrong if I didn't hear the f-bomb from you at least once in a conversation."

"Oh good, because that's fucking hard to hold back." Katie sighed with relief.

Schultz took in a breath and leaned back, looking around the restaurant. "It's hard to believe just a couple of weeks, maybe less, you could find a demon anywhere. Now? Church mice. They're all hiding out."

Pandora cleared the ravioli from her throat. *They are probably just harder to find. Most up this way don't think it can happen to them, you know? They can't imagine running into a merc like you. The rest are the smart ones, hiding out until things go back to normal.*

I'm hoping this is the new normal.

Pandora chuckled. *Yeah, it's a pipe dream. I can promise you Moloch is only getting started.*

Great. Just great.

Schultz pursed his lips. He stole a glance at Travers. The other man shifted in his seat nervously. Travers put his hands in his lap and leaned back. "I want to ask a question."

Uh-oh.

Katie swallowed another big bite of ravioli and assented. "Sure, go ahead."

Travers shuffled nervously. "During a meeting about your tracking device, it was mentioned that Pandora really liked Batman. We were just wondering if she was still into superheroes?"

Katie grinned and put up her finger. "I think that is a question for Pandora."

Go ahead, Katie told Pandora.

Pandora squealed. She gathered herself and took over Katie's body, although she left her looks the same so as not to disturb the people around them. Pandora sat up straighter in her chair and pulled the napkin into her lap. She held her fork daintily and continuing to eat in a somewhat refined manner. If she hadn't been eating in double-time, one would never know anything had changed.

Pandora swallowed a bite and took a sip of her wine, then retrieved her napkin with two fingers and blotted her lips. "I have to admit, the whole rumor about superheroes and me? It's true. In my mind, superheroes are the closest things to heroes from the old days. Of course, those heroes were a bit different. They didn't wear capes or masks. Oh, some did, but it wasn't a whole thing. They didn't jump from tall buildings or fly around either. They did the things that were morally right for the people in their lives, and their societies."

The detectives looked back and forth at each other, surprised to hear this from a demon. Pandora didn't seem to notice. She just continued talking.

"During that nasty war, the one in the forties where they killed all those Jewish people, I met the nicest man. He knew if he stood up to the Nazis and attempted to help the Jewish people, they would shoot him dead. I sat him down in Poland at this neat little deli that was eventually taken over by the Germans. We had these delightful cheese perogies. Anyway. I told him if you can't save them all, save as many as you can. It was like a lightbulb went off for him."

Travers narrowed his eyes and tilted his head. "Wait. Are you talking about…"

Pandora swallowed and glanced at Travers. "Oskar Schindler? Yes. Anyway, from there he started to bring Jewish people into his factories. He was able to pull from the concentration camps and put them to work. Those people didn't end up in the ovens. In the end, I heard he saved, like, over a thousand people. Compared to the millions who were killed it seems like a small number, but it wasn't small to those people."

Travers sputtered, "But you're a demon."

"One of the things demons do constantly is play both sides of the fence. They do whatever it takes to get what they want."

Schultz's mouth dropped open, and he shook his head. "That's an incredible story."

Pandora didn't even blink. "The whole point of it was, he was a hero. He might not have been called superhero because he didn't have any type of magical abilities, but to me, that's what a hero is."

When she was done with her story, the two detectives sat there for several moments in silence, just watching her eat. After a bit of time had passed, Schultz looked at Travers and nodded. Travers pulled out what seemed to be a small men's leather wallet and slid it across the table to Pandora.

Pandora flipped the case open. A golden badge rested on the leather. Her jaw dropped, revealing half-chewed ravioli. "What's this?"

Schultz smiled. "We don't want you to go vigilante. Try not to kill anyone."

Travers piped in, "Unless they're demons."

"Right. Demons excluded."

Pandora closed her mouth and swallowed, then picked up the badge with both hands like it was some delicate flower. She tilted it back and forth, watching the light play across its surface. They had made her a real superhero, at least on paper. She pursed her lips and looked at the men. She blinked and quickly grabbed her napkin to wipe away a welling tear. They had really gone above and beyond to make her feel important, something people had rarely done for her in the past.

Well shit, you take back over. You know I can't handle this mushy shit, Pandora blubbered to Katie.

I got you.

Katie came back into her body and put the napkin down on her plate. She sniffed at the two detectives. "That was really nice of you guys to do that for Pandora. I have to admit, she was so touched that she didn't know how to handle it. She sent me back out."

Pandora scoffed. *I know how to handle good touching.*

Travers and Schultz stood up, Schultz reaching into his pocket and pulling out a long gold chain. He handed it to Katie. "This is for her to attach to the case. Anyway, we're glad you liked it. We're going to let you get back to your meal."

Katie took a deep breath and pushed her plate away. "I won't be far behind you. I've had my fill for tonight, and I think Pandora's done."

The detectives smiled kindly at her and walked out of the restaurant. A moment later the waitress came to the table bearing espresso and tiramisu. "From the two gentle-men," she explained.

Katie chuckled to herself as she ate, Pandora silent inside her. After all the things her demon had seen and done, having people be nice to her was the one true way to shock Pandora into silence. Katie was starting to think

Pandora was going soft, but she would never say that to her.

Katie collected her things and headed out of the restaurant, stopping on the busy sidewalk and stretching her arms over her head. Droves of cars raced by on the New York City streets, and there were people everywhere, locals and tourists alike.

You better hail us a cab, Pandora snapped without a thought.

I can do better than that.

Pandora perked up. *What are you talking about?*

Katie smirked and took off running, straight toward a large truck moving slowly down the block.

8

___

Katie leaped over cars and dodged swerving bicyclists, running as fast as she could to catch up with the truck. The whole time, a mischievous smile was plastered on her face.

___

"This broadcast is brought to you today by Reims Insurance. Nobody can deny that the world is a different place today than it was even two years ago. Paranormal and abnormal activity is now rampant. On today's show, we're going to delve into the effects that activity has on society," the radio host announced with a chuckle.

Adam shifted in his seat excitedly and turned up the radio. He loved the show. The over-the-top blowhard radio host and his rhetoric made for good listening while he drove his rig around town. He also appreciated the informational aspects of the show. He thought it was important to keep up with what was going on in current events, namely the demons and various incursions.

The radio host continued, "I'm just gonna put this out there because you know I don't bullshit my listeners. I think a lot of this demon shit is overhyped. Like with any of the other times in our history. One minute there's some crazy virus going around the world, the next we've got a radical group that *they* say is endangering the entire country. It's *all* overhyped. The government wants everyone to believe that the outside world is detrimental to our health and that we should stay in our homes, bolt our doors, and hide like good little peons."

The truck driver chuckled. "Maybe you should take a walk on the New York streets once in a while."

"And don't even get me started on these fake fucking videos about Katie from Katie's Killers. As if that little girl has ever killed one soul. I bet she's never even stomped on a bug." The radio host laughed, and Adam chuckled along with him.

The host was on a roll. He had found a good subject, and like a dog with a new toy, he was going to go after it. "Besides, how is someone that freaking hot a killer? That never happens, not outside the movies. If a girl like that truly was being chased by all these damn demons, there would be a hundred guys lined up at her door to protect her. *They* needed to slap a face onto the war on demons, so they picked the prettiest one they could find."

Adam snorted laughter and reached into the passenger seat to grab a hot dog wrapped in tinfoil. He kept one hand on the steering wheel as he unwrapped the hot dog and took a big bite. Ketchup and mustard shot from the other end and ran down his shirt. "Shit!"

He put the hot dog back down on the seat and went to grab a napkin. His eyes bounced from the road in front of him to the mustard on his shirt. He shook his head and wiped at the condiments, really only smearing them around. Adam grumbled, "Fuck it" and grabbed the hot dog again, taking another big bite. His eyes drifted to the road and grew wide.

Katie—*the* Katie from Katie's Killers—was running straight at his slow-moving truck.

He dropped the hot dog in his lap and grabbed the steering wheel, hitting the brakes. "Holy shit!"

Katie looked straight at him as she ran forward and jumped up, planting both feet on the truck's front bumper. She gave him one of her signature smiles and launched straight up into the air, out of sight.

Adam slammed both feet on the brake pedal and the truck came to a screeching halt. He leaned as far out the window as he could. He could see her wings opening on each side of her body, and then the woman flew into the sky.

He couldn't believe what he was seeing, Katie from Katie's killers right in front of him. He had seen a lot of shit in New York, but he hadn't had a Katie sighting yet. In fact, it had been on his list. He wanted to see her, and he had planned to go out next time he heard about an incursion just so he could watch her at work. Luckily for him, he didn't have to go far. There she was, wings and all, right above his head.

Adam slid back into his seat and searched frantically for his phone. "They aren't going to fucking believe this."

He grabbed his phone and hit speed dial. On the radio, he could hear the host still going on about how Katie was fake and how the videos were made to look worse than what they really were. "It's a false flag, just like everything else in this world. New York seems to be the center of it, maybe because there are so many people. Oh! Looks like our weekly caller from New York City is on the line. Let's hear from Big Adam from the Big Apple."

Adam fumbled with this phone and turned down the radio to reduce feedback. He started to laugh nervously, still not believing what he just saw. "I'm going to tell you right now, I think you're a dumbass for not believing the hype. I live in New York City, and I see shit every day. When's the last time you went out to one of these incursions or walked the streets of the boroughs?"

The radio host started laughing sarcastically. "What happened? Are you a video expert now, Big Adam? Because last time I talked to you, I could've sworn you were a truck driver in New York. Then again, these days most people are experts on something outside of their normal range of work."

Adam scoffed. "No, I'm not a video expert, but I do believe what I see with my own eyes."

"Okay, so you've seen Katie from Katie's Killers? And I don't mean on one of those sexy billboards in Times Square, Big Adam. I'm talking about in the flesh, huge tits, giant guns on her hips, and flaring red eyes. I'm talking about where you could reach out and touch her if she wouldn't bite your fucking hand off."

Adam picked up his hot dog and took a bite, talking while he was chewing. "I have. In fact, I just saw her. I was driving along in my truck, and what do I see? I'll tell you what. Katie, running at full speed toward my truck and then leaping off the bumper and flying into the sky with those huge angel wings. So unless there's something in my afternoon hot dog, I seen Katie from Katie's Killers. And I saw this with my Mark One eyeball, the best bullshit detector I have."

Nila shut the front door of the apartment and walked down the stairs. She sat down on the bottom step and sighed wishing she could go back to school and continue studying her sixth-grade science. It had been a long time since she actually enjoyed being at home, especially with her brother and her mother fighting all the time. She was despondent, looking straight down at the ground and not even blinking.

From the outside, no one could really tell what was on her mind. Was she suicidal? No, but she had some weighty things on her mind, especially for a girl her age. She was sad; really sad. She wished her brother would stop being such a dummy.

The sound of her mother's voice rang out from behind the closed doors. "I just wish that you would appreciate the fact that I'm trying to raise you the best that I can. I don't work my rear end off so that you can go run the streets at night and get yourself into this much trouble!"

Her brother snapped back. "I'm almost an adult. I can

make my own decisions! It's not my fault you're gone all the time. I get bored."

Her mother scoffed. "Oh, okay. If you're such an adult, why don't you go out and get a damn job? Why don't you study a little bit harder and get good grades in school so you can get into college? If you want to be an adult, then you need to start acting like one instead of acting like a spoiled little child, because I didn't raise you that way!"

Nila put her hands over her ears and stared down at the street. A lone leaf skittered past her, following by several pebbles rolling along. A sudden wind picked up, kicking dust into her eyes. Over the wind, she heard a huge thumping sound, like a big heart beating—or like mighty wings flapping. She squinted around, but didn't see anything. She lifted her head and her mouth fell open. Carefully descending to the street in front of her was Katie, her large wings spread wide.

Nila was shocked to see Katie in real life. She had seen her on the television several times, but it never seemed real. Katie folded her wings behind her and tilted her head toward Nila.

Katie nodded at the door. "Hi. May I go in?"

Nila looked behind her at the sounds of her mother and brother fighting. "My brother. He's not a demon, just a dumbass."

Katie laughed and put her hands on her hips. "Most guys are at that age. Then again, moms don't always react well to kids growing up."

Katie touched down and walked over next to Nila. The girl reached toward her wings, but by the time her fingers got close they had disappeared.

Pandora snapped inside Katie's head, *You don't touch the wings! That's like touching the coochie without any smoochy. It's just damn rude.*

Katie frowned, not sure why Pandora was so bent out of shape about a young girl touching her wings. *All right, calm down, demon lady. She's just a child.*

If you don't teach them young, they end up like that little shitbird inside. Manners. It's all about manners.

Katie chuckled. *That's rich, coming from you.*

Katie didn't give Pandora a chance to respond. She knew it would be something smart, anyway. She studied Nila and took a knee in front of her. "I promise it'll be okay. Things like this tend to work themselves out eventually. I'm just gonna go in and see if I can't help a little bit, all right?"

Nila nodded and watched as Katie walked up the stairs and opened the front door.

Katie went inside and looked around the meagerly-furnished house. It was apparent that the woman was a single mom doing the best she could.

The mother snapped her head to the doorway. "Nila! Don't you have homework?"

Katie walked into the kitchen and smiled. The woman's look of surprise turned into recognition, and she cleared her throat and stepped back. Katie's eyes shifted from the mother to the son, sizing them up. She crossed her arms over her chest, and the boy glared at her indignantly.

Katie thought about the two of them, then chuckled and grabbed the boy by the arm. She said to the mother, "I'll take this." Then to the boy, "There's something I want to show you."

The boy was only about sixteen, so it wasn't hard for Katie to manhandle him. The kid clearly did not like that. The mother was too stunned to say anything, and she merely watched as Katie walked him over to the window. "Look outside."

The boy puffed out his chest and tried to shrug her off, but Katie could tell he was scared. He snarled, "C'mon. Seen it a hundred times, what's going to be so unique about one hundred and one?"

Katie grabbed the kid under the arms. "This…"

She pushed him through the window and over the side of the fire escape. The kid screamed as he fell.

"No! Don't hurt him! He's not a demon. I love him!" the mother yelled after Katie.

Katie dove after the boy and caught him. Between his screaming and the mom yelling, Katie was starting to think that she made a bad decision.

Katie's wings instantly popped out, and they flew skyward. Nila ran to her mother, and they scrambled to the window to watch them fly off. Nila patted her mother on the shoulder. "Mom, calm down. She knows he's not a demon. I talked to her. Just take a deep breath. I promise you, when she gets back, things will be different."

The mother nodded her head and pulled Nila close. They stood there for only about ten minutes, but to the mother, it seemed like hours. Finally, they saw Katie approach, carrying the teen in her arms. Nila noticed almost immediately that the boy was smiling. Katie hovered over the fire escape and dropped him the last foot. He scrambled through the window and hugged his mom tightly before she could say a word.

The boy began to ramble. "I'm sorry. I'm sorry about before. And I'm sorry we were gone so long too, I was looking for jobs…"

The mother sniffled happily and hugged him again. He continued apologizing, and together they walked deeper into the house.

Nila climbed out onto the fire escape and grabbed the railing. Katie hovered in front of her and gave her a warm, comforting grin. "Want to see what the city looks like from above? I've gotta get back home, but I can spare a few minutes."

Nila peeked inside. Her mother and brother were sitting in the living room, and they weren't paying any attention to her. She climbed up on the railing and jumped toward Katie. Katie caught her and squeezed her tightly, then flapped her wings in great heartbeat-like thumps as they ascended.

Far below them on a street corner, for just a moment, a man thought he heard two girls giggling, accompanied by the steady rhythmic beat of angel wings.

9

Timothy rolled his office chair across the IT room, humming to himself happily. Everything was in order, just the way he liked it. Now that he had an actual job instead of just looking for random things and keeping the base safe, he had relaxed. It also helped that Korbin and Stephanie were back. Timothy and Stephanie had picked up like they were never apart.

"I'm grabbing some sandwiches. You want one?" Stephanie asked, poking her head in the door.

Timothy raised his hands in submission. "Girl, I'm getting fatter by the minute. If I'm not careful, I won't fit into those leather Louis dress pants I bought the other day. Gotta keep my tummy small and my fanny tight."

Stephanie laughed. "Okay, I'll check on you later."

Timothy pursed his lips. "Kisses!"

He rolled over to the main computer to take notes on some system updates that he had been working on. Everything was going perfectly. The system was working just as promised, and the cops couldn't be happier. On top of that, he had probably saved hundreds of lives by creating his software. It was a win-win all around...except for the demons.

He wrote down the last of his notes and closed his book. He looked around the empty room, then leaned back and put his arms behind his head. "It's good to be the boss. Well, kind of the boss." He thought about that for a second. "And kind-of bosses deserve iced coffee."

Timothy grabbed his wallet and headed for the door. He was internally debating the pros and cons of mocha versus vanilla when one of the alarms went off. This happened quite often, and it was effortless to take care of. Nothing to be worried about. He leaned over his desk and read the information on the screen, and his eyes grew wide. His wallet dropped from his hand and hit the desk, all thoughts of a frozen mocha gone.

"Holy shit," he whispered to no one, then grabbed the phone and fumbled with the buttons on the intercom until he finally got it. He knew he'd done it right because the speakers throughout the entire underground base started screeching loudly. He held the receiver to his mouth and tried to calm his nerves. "Calvin, we have a code red. Shit, we have a code red and a *half*. Get the fuck down here."

Calvin was close. Timothy heard a door open and heavy footsteps pound as the other man ran down the hall toward his area. More steps followed as somebody else, who turned out to be Korbin, ran into the room. Calvin was breathing heavily, and he put his hand on the doorframe for support. Timothy looked at him with concern. "Did I interrupt something?"

Calvin waved the comment away. "I'm not quite in the best shape right now. What you got?"

Timothy jerked his hand toward the screen. "Oh, nothing. Just that we have a new portal—a really fucking big one. It's opening a half a mile from here."

Korbin narrowed his eyes and peered over Timothy's shoulder, studying the screen. Calvin immediately called the general.

When the general answered, it sounded like he was chewing something. "General Brushwood."

Calvin cleared his throat. "General, we have a code red. A new portal opening just a half a mile away from us. From what Timothy says it's a motherfucking huge one."

The general coughed and fumbled with something in front of him, making a loud noise over the phone. "Okay, got it. I'll call Nellis for support, then get the plane scrambled and my people on this one. I would appreciate your backup."

"Of course. We'll see you there…or here. Whatever."

Calvin shut the phone and sent Katie a text.

Huge incursion on the radar just a half a mile from us, but sit tight. We don't know what's going on. We don't want to play into the demons' hands if they're trying to get you away from New York.

Katie was sitting comfortably on her couch watching Batman for the three hundredth time when her phone started to buzz. She pulled her phone out and leisurely read through the text, gradually sitting up straighter. When she finished reading her body was ramrod straight. Angie sat up with her, waiting for her cue.

Katie's stare shifted around the room for a moment as she thought. Her eyes landed on Angie. "I want you to get my plane ready. And by ready, I mean loaded with any weapons I can't fit on my body and all the extra ammunition I have."

Angie agreed and ran from the living room. Katie had planned to go out after she was done watching Batman, and was already dressed in her battle gear, with her guns strapped to her hips and knives stashed all over. She figured Angie would get the rest of it for her. She took a big gulp of her drink and set it down on the coffee table, stopping for a moment to grab a coaster and put it underneath.

Pandora scoffed. *Boy, have you changed. There's a major incursion, and you take the time to put a fucking coaster underneath your drink.*

Katie shrugged her shoulders as she walked toward the window. *Hey, when the incursion's done, we still have to come here. I don't want to come back to rings on my coffee table.*

Snobby bitch, Pandora grumbled.

Katie ignored her and walked to the window, and with no hesitation, she opened it and jumped out. Her wings spread wide, and she soared into the sky and headed to the airport. Flying there would be faster than catching a cab. The last thing she needed was to be stuck in traffic.

Angie stood at the window and watched as Katie flew toward the airport. She had the phone pressed to her ear and was waiting for the coordinator to get back on the line. When he did, she snapped, "FYI, you guys might want to hurry."

She could hear him typing, and the guy let out a yawn. "Traffic sucks right now, so we have at least an hour. Unless she gets police support?"

Angie scoffed. "Traffic's not a problem when you have wings."

The guy choked and coughed before yelling, "We need this done in fifteen minutes if not faster! Katie will be here any second. I don't have time to mess with you fools. Move your feet!"

He came back to the phone and softened his tone. "We'll be ready."

Angie chuckled and hung up. There was a knock at the door, and when she opened it, she saw the doorman standing there. Angie smiled at him. "I don't need you to run anything over there today. All the weapons she needs will be on her plane. Besides, unless you have wings hidden under that uniform, there's no way you'll make it there before her."

The doorman smirked and gave her a slight bow turning back down the hallway. Angie shut the door and leaned against it, thinking about how strange her life had gotten since the fateful day Katie saved her. She had to admit, a pair of wings just might've helped her in that situation. Being part angel might have given her enough protection from her douchebag ex-boyfriend that she could have gotten out of there on her own.

Angie shrugged. "Then I wouldn't be here, and I wouldn't have this awesome-sauce job."

"Move it! Move it!" The staff at the airport was hustling like they never had before.

Stacks upon stacks of ammunition were loaded onto the plane one by one and strapped down to ensure that they didn't go flying off. Piles of weapons were already tied down inside, as well as the new technology that Joshua had sent over earlier that month. Katie had managed to get the airport to agree to give her a secured area where she could store all of her equipment and not have to transport it back and forth every time she wanted to take the plane.

One of the staff members stopped for a moment and leaned against a box of ammunition. She dug out a rag and wiped her forehead. "Jesus, you would think she was already here and had been waiting for hours. It's not like planes load themselves. It takes time."

One of the other staff members grabbed a crate of ammo. "Sure, sure. Except I think you're forgetting we're dealing with Katie from Katie's Killers. You know, the one with angel wings and a demon inside? I don't really think she gives a damn if it takes time. All she's thinking about is saving whoever's in trouble. You can't blame her for that."

The girl nodded. "I guess you're right. And I'm the last person who wants to be caught slacking in front of Katie. I like my head where it is."

The guy chuckled. "The feeling is mutual, my friend."

They loaded the last three boxes of ammunition onto the plane and began to start bringing up the weapons. The girl turned to grab a gun and saw something through the bay doors. She cursed. "It's her!"

Everyone stopped and stared as Katie flew in. She hovered in the air for a moment and slowly and carefully landed on the pavement. It was still crazy to watch as her massive wings folded behind her and then disappeared. Katie shook her head and rolled her shoulders, which were sore from having flown so much that day.

She took a deep breath and started walking toward the bay, then noticed everyone staring at her. She stared right back at them, then clapped her hands. "Let's go, people! This bird needs to get in the air!"

With that, everyone jumped to it. They all started moving even faster than they had been before. The stairs were down, so Katie walked right up and into the cabin. The pilot was strapped and ready. The flight attendant appeared from nowhere with a box of donuts and set them next to Katie.

Katie glanced at the donuts and then at the flight attendant. "She didn't ask for them, so it doesn't go against the pact we made."

The flight attendant smiled as she walked away, even though she didn't know what Katie was talking about.

Snack in a fucking minute if they don't get this plane off the ground, Pandora barked.

The portal ripped across the horizon like a foul, warped bolt of lightning. It could be likened to what flesh tearing and bones cracking might sound like to the humans. Heat bellowed out of the open portal, and demons began to emerge one by one. They reached their clawed feet into the world like hideous newborns, then pulled themselves over the edge of the portal to drop snarling onto the ground.

They emerged from the portal by the hundreds, tripping over one other and kicking and biting and clawing at each other as they flooded onto the field. They had been instructed where to go, but they weren't the brightest crayons in the box. It took them a minute to find the building they were supposed to be surrounding.

When they did, they took off in a hurry, pushing each other out of the way and scrambling for the fence that surrounded the building. They clawed over the fence, some of them getting caught up in the concertina on the top. The more intellectually challenged demons bit and slashed their own legs off to free themselves from the wire. Others took the smarter route, using their claws to rip great holes in the fence line and pour through.

In the distance, a group of humans stood watching them, screaming at the horror of it all.

Normally this would have grabbed the demons' attention since they were always looking for a good excuse for a snack, but not this time. They were on a mission, and they knew that their leader was not going to accept any digressions, even if it were for a tasty arm or foot. There would be plenty of carnage to satisfy them later. They just had to reach their destination and ready themselves for the battle. None of them really had any idea what was coming.

Through the portal were two of the great horrors of hell. Just inside the gate stood Moloch and Baal. They sat around a large table, laughing as the demons fell through the gate and fumbled around below. The little guys were incredibly stupid, but they would do the job that needed to be done.

Moloch grabbed one of the leftover turtles from the night before and popped it into his mouth. "I have to admit, they may be stupid, but they're fun to watch. I just don't know if they're going to be the best tool for this job. We have to use so many of them, and in the end, there's not even an assurance that it *will* get done. We've seen it over and over. These little idiot demons get taken down in two seconds by the mercs."

Baal wiped turtle fluids from his chin, then cracked a splinter of shell from one of the dead turtles and picked his teeth with it. "I know. Remember, we're only using the lesser demons to test the defenses. We don't actually expect them to do anything. Once we know what their defenses are, we'll up the efforts."

Moloch cracked his knuckles and grinned evilly. "That's right. That's when we bring out the big guns. I can't wait to see the look on that meatsack's face when our heavy artillery comes plowing through. I'm tired of these mercs thinking they can get one over on us using just a little bit of technology. All it took was two idiots willing to sell their souls for me to get the location of the weapons."

They both laughed loudly as they watched one of the demons do a somersault into the next. "Did you see that motherfucking idiot? He just pulled a Mary Lou Retton! Out there on the field doing a double somersault backflip." Baal shook his head, amazed.

Moloch bellowed and grabbed a piece of burning red rock from the floor and used his claw to scratch into it. He held the rock high in the air and waved it at the gate. He had scratched a burning score, *nine-point-five,* into the stone. "That's right little demons! Go for gold."

10

The demons clawed their way across the sandy ground, sniffing out humans. There weren't a lot of tall buildings on the base, so it wasn't hard to find the weaponry building. They just looked for the most populated area and scrambled that way.

Unbeknownst to them, the demons had set an alarm off when they breached the fence.

Joshua hit the button, acknowledging he'd heard the thing. He grabbed several weapons from the arms cabinet behind his desk and tossed one to a woman standing nearby. She nodded in understanding. It was time to fight, or at least get the others to safety. With the incursion appearing so close to the base, it was no surprise that they were headed straight for them.

Joshua and the others were hell-bent on protecting the base, remembering full well what kind of damage the demons had done when they'd attacked their last installation. Outside, the underground cannons began thundering at the guard station. The guards shouldered their weapons and began to fire at the oncoming demons. They were ripping the fences apart, but that wasn't too surprising.

One of the guards took careful aim, exhaled, and pulled the trigger, sending a bullet straight into a crowd of demons. A horned head exploded into ash. The man looked back at the scared young guard behind him. The first guard blew a plume of smoke from his gun barrel. "Get it the fuck together and take out as many of these cocksuckers as you can. We're the first line of defense."

Through the gate to hell, Moloch and Baal sat watching. They were pretty impressed by the way the humans were protecting their base.

Moloch nodded and crunched down on another snack, something that wiggled and squealed as he gnashed his teeth through it. "Look at those contraptions they've made. I have to say, they may have learned from the last incursion."

Baal laughed. "I do believe they have. I would have to say their defenses are excellent. Got pop-up guns ready and loaded. They have traps, which I haven't seen used on a demon before, but look! That pit full of sharpened stakes keeps catching the little idiots. And they're setting mines off right and left."

The two demons watched as a group of lesser demons ran across the sandy ground. One moment they were running full-speed, the next they had been blown sky-high in ragged pieces. Baal gestured at the clearing smoke. "See? Mine."

Another group of demons ran from the explosion, collapsing through a false floor and into a pit of sharpened stakes. Some burst into ash, but others were only wounded. They snarled in pain and growled when one of the security guards walked up to the trap. He leveled his gun at them with a smirk. "Not as easy as you thought, huh?"

The red eyes of the demons blazed, and their sharp teeth dripped with saliva. They began pulling themselves from the stakes and climbing out of the pit. The guard grimaced and sent a spray of bullets into the trap, turning all of them to ash. Then he reset the trap, and the false floor slid back into place. He chuckled, knowing full well that the next demons wouldn't be smart enough to avoid it.

Joshua shifted his eyes to the girl he had handed the weapon to. "Get the women to the underground bunkers. You know the routine. The hatch's right over there, inside the vault."

She acknowledged that nervously and ran off, collecting anyone who wasn't staying to fight. They headed into the vault, and she led them down through the hatch and locked it after them.

Joshua slammed his hand on an emergency button on his desk and then listened. Gears in the building began to turn, and there was the sound of metal sliding as steel blast guards began to cover the production building. They would make sure that the building was secure during any kind of fight.

Joshua checked his weapon and stared angrily at the front door. He knew he had to stay and protect the building, no matter what. He wanted to fight, but Katie and the others wouldn't have it. He was the only one who knew how to fabricate the weapons, and that made him the most valuable person on the entire base.

Calvin bolted through the underground tunnels toward the training room where the weapons were stashed. He grabbed his boots out of the locker and hopped on one foot at a time as he put them on. Stephanie and Korbin came around the corner and froze, watching him.

Calvin stopped hopping and gestured to the racks of guns along the wall. "All of these weapons are made for the special bullets that we manufacture. They work just like any other weapon, but they are especially lethal when you are fighting demons" Calvin strapped two guns into his holsters and slid two long swords into the sheaths he'd strapped to his back.

Korbin squeezed Stephanie's hand and looked at her lovingly. "Don't wait for us, but we *will* be there."

Calvin stopped his weapons check and shook Korbin's hand. "It's good to have you back."

Korbin smirked. "It might sound strange—hell, it sounds strange to me!—but it feels good to be back, even if I'm not really sure what that means."

Calvin patted Korbin on the back and ran for the elevator. Korbin and Stephanie admired the weapons for a moment, then Stephanie looked at him and he pulled her in for a fierce kiss. Stephanie broke it off. "All right, let's get to work."

Stephanie pulled her sweatshirt off, leaving her in a tight black tank top and black spandex pants. Korbin hadn't moved. He was staring at her. Stephanie wagged her finger. "Time for that later. Now, move." Korbin grabbed his gear and began to suit up.

She pulled a pair of boots on. "Hey, these fit pretty well."

Korbin chuckled as he laced his up. "Hell, they might've been yours."

Stephanie pulled on a double holster and grabbed two pistols, putting one in each side. She walked over to the daggers and chose four of them. "I feel like I could definitely do some damage with these." She stuck them in sheaths on her Kevlar vest and flexed, testing her range of motion.

Korbin was staring at her. "I feel like you probably could."

She shrugged her shoulders and grinned. "Do as the Romans do."

Korbin laughed and stuck a long fat-bladed knife into a sheath on his side. "Damn right."

Calvin passed the elevator and skidded to a stop in the IT room. Timothy was wheeling his chair around the room. He was a one-man whirlwind, typing here, checking a screen there around the room. He stopped and looked at Calvin. "The weapons production building should be completely locked down. Josh is inside, ready to fight if he needs to, and many of the girls are working their way through to the bunker. As soon as they clear the doors, I'll lock it down."

The merc nodded. "Good. Keep checking with us, just in case we need anything from down here. I'm pretty sure we have all we need up there, but you never know. There could be more demons than we know what to do with. It might be a little while before the military shows up."

Timothy tapped his ear. "My earpiece is good to go. I'm just waiting for everybody to turn on theirs. I made sure Korbin and Stephanie had one this morning. For some reason, I just had a bad feeling. I'll run communication from in here. I can seal the room if I need to be locked completely inside. Get to it. I'll flip any switches you need, just let me know."

One of the guards came over the loudspeaker. "The first wave is over, but we can see the rest coming. I'm not sure how many more waves there are."

Calvin grabbed the walkie on his shoulder and pressed the button. "Ten-four. We are on our way up to the surface. Just hold them for us and we'll help you as soon as we get there. Have you taken heavy casualties?"

The guard replied. "Just one. These demons aren't the brightest."

Calvin chuckled. "They never are. Hold it down, buddy. We're coming."

Calvin turned to leave the room and ran smack into Korbin and Stephanie. They were all decked out in their battle gear. It made Calvin think of old times, back when they'd headed into incursions together, and he couldn't help but smile. He shifted his eyes to the floor.

Korbin walked over to the security monitors that pointed at the yard. "They said they're coming in waves?"

Timothy took a deep breath and pressed a button so he could see the entirety of the grounds. "They say the first round is over, but they don't know how many are coming. From the size of the portal and its proximity to us, we could be looking at one of the largest incursions to date."

Korbin shook his head. "I don't think they're here to attack, or at least they're not here to take anything from us. They're testing us. I've seen it on the battlefield a hundred times. They want to know our defenses, so that when they send in the big guns, they're prepared."

Timothy typed a command into his computer. "I'm not going to let them get through. I don't care what kind of demons they send. We spent countless man-hours working on the defense plot you set up with Calvin. It's impenetrable. Well, it's at least *really* good at keeping the demons away from what's important. I've made some adjustments and added some technology so I can control everything from this desk."

Korbin looked at all the keys and buttons. "Is this the only place it can be controlled from?"

Timothy let out a puff of air. "Please, bitch, there is no way I would leave all the controls in one spot. I know I'm a hacker and not a soldier, but I do have some brains. Everything can be controlled from here, yes. I also set up an emergency control room at the guard station, and one in the armory. Those two rooms are a lot simpler; they just have basic controls. From here I can adjust height, power, and even reload anything that needs it without having to actually go down there and do it."

Korbin was impressed. "Nice job. I'm sure you were an asset to this team even when I was here. It looks like you guys have things under control."

Calvin chuckled and patted him on the shoulder. "We have things locked up tight, now that you and Stephanie are here with us. We know what kind of badassery the two of you can put out. Each of you fights like a dozen civilians. Now all we need is for the military to get here and help us out, especially with the air assault."

As if in response to the comment, the whole bunker shook, and dust rained from the ceiling. Calvin squinted against the dust and grinned at the others. "The planes are dropping bombs on the incursion area. That's good news because it means the military's close."

Near the portal, a squad of sleek bombers roared over-head. Missiles fell onto the mass of demons below, killing hundreds of demons at a time. The bombers turned and made another pass, but the demons kept coming. No matter how many they killed, more came out.

Moloch leaned out the gate to watch as another plane flew by. His elbow jostled his chalice, and he grabbed the cup of blood so it wouldn't tip over.

Baal took a sip from his own chalice as bombs blew the lesser demons apart and chuckled, causing bright blood to spill down his chin. "Well, it looks like the military has arrived."

Another explosion hit, this one rocking the ground beneath Moloch's and Baal's feet. Dirt and rocks pelted the two demons through the gate. They both howled, furious that they were being disturbed as they tried to relax and watch the fight. They took a few steps backward, pulling the table with them, and sat back down to continue watching.

Moloch flicked a stone from the table and leaned back in his chair. "I have to admit, this is much more resistance than I thought we would see."

Baal nodded his head. "True. But I think when we pull out the Big One we won't have any problem taking down most of this."

Moloch glared at him and then back at the gate. "Just remember, she's not here yet. We don't know how much damage she'll do when she arrives."

Baal flicked his large claws dismissively. "I know she's a tough bitch, but we are tough, too. We will not make the same mistake that we made last time."

The portal was opposite the landing pad. The demons continued spilling out at a rapid pace and spread over the entire killing field. They knew what their target was, and they knew they had to be fast to get where they were going. What they didn't realize was that the mercs had already thought out every possible battle scenario.

A grizzled guard pointed to slits in the metal blast shield surrounding the production building. "Take a hole, men, and aim well."

The men stepped to the slits, resting their guns on the edge of the blast shield. There were over thirty of them high in the production building, and when the grizzled guard roared, "Fire!" they rained their own brand of hell upon the killing field. Dozens of demons went down one after another, squawking and howling before they crumbled into dust. The grizzled guard had been practicing his aim, and every bullet he fired found a grotesque face and turned a demon to ash.

They went through a massive number of bullets, but they had more than enough to keep firing. The reports of their guns could be heard for miles. It sounded like a war zone right there outside Las Vegas. As the second wave began to slow, so did the shooters. Piles of dust floated in the wind toward the mountains.

A few straggling demons scrambled through the dust clouds that had been their comrades and skirted through the gunfire, still intent on making their way to the armored building.

The grizzled guard peered down at them, reloading as they spat and growled, scratching the blast shield that protected the building. He removed his combat helmet and tipped it over the edge and it hit a snarling demon in the head. The thing looked at him with its beady red eyes and roared, and the guard aimed between those red eyes and pulled the trigger.

The demon went down in a burst of dust, and the grizzled guy laughed and pulled back from the slit. He shook his head at the other soldiers. "They've made it to the building, so I need you to take down as many as you can before they start climbing. They may be dumb, but they can see that there is a way in. We cannot let a single demon into this building. We also can't let them know there are ways in *even* when the shield is active. This is what we've been waiting for, boys, so let's get it done!"

11

Timothy took a deep breath and pressed the phone to his ear. "The portal is huge. It stretches hundreds of feet behind the landing pad. The demons are coming in waves, and Korbin believes they're testing us, or testing our defenses, at least. Calvin, Korbin, and Stephanie are out in the field taking down demons before they can get to the weapons building. The shield is active, and it's holding for now. The building guards are at battle stations, picking off demons in the killing field, but several have gotten through. They're now at the production building, trying to figure out how to get in."

Katie was worried that she wasn't going to get there in time. "And they can't pick those off too?"

"No, they are out of their line of sight because of the shield. They're doing their best, though. As soon as one starts to climb, they take it down. The next wave should be coming soon. We have air support now and they've started bombing the portal, but it doesn't seem to be making any difference. The heat is so intense that it's fried some of the circuits in the field, and we're experiencing some malfunctioning. Nothing major, though. *Yet.*"

Katie had never even thought about that part of it. "Shit. Okay, I'll be there as soon as I can. We are close."

Katie hung up and let her mind settle for a moment before looking at the cockpit door. She unbuckled her seatbelt, hurried through the cabin, and knocked once before opening it. The pilot looked at her. "We're almost there, Katie. I'm going as fast as I can."

She put her hand on the pilot's shoulder. "I know you are. Apparently, the portal is really close to the landing pad, so you might need to… *Shit.* Actually, you can see it ahead of you in the distance."

The pilot leaned forward and narrowed his eyes. The great portal that stretched across the horizon hung directly over the landing strip. "Well, that's unfortunate."

Katie agreed, but there weren't a lot of other options for her to get close fast. "I know it's close, but do you think you can land? You don't even have to completely touchdown. I can jump out as you taxi in. Just slow down, and then you can take right off again. The only thing is that you *have* to slow down enough for me to jump. Even with my wings, if you're going too fast, I'll tumble and possibly even be sucked into the engine."

The copilot grabbed the information booklet on the landing strip. "We wouldn't want that to happen, now would we?"

He immediately started doing the calculations to figure out the best speed for them to come in at so she could jump out and survive the landing. Katie waited patiently. Ahead, the lights on the landing strip near the base grew larger and larger. It almost looked like they led right to the portal and on into hell. The copilot finished writing and tapped his pen against his lips, then showed his work to the captain.

The captain looked at the figures for a second and then at Katie. "We're not sure if we can slow the plane enough for you to get out safely. I'm sure that I can do a dip and take off again before I hit the portal, but like I said, I don't know about the speed."

Calvin had come back inside to check on Timothy, but he had only made it into the training area. The weapons and ammo cache had caught his eye, and he decided he could use a reload. He sighed as he put several clips on his belt and grabbed another dagger. He had lost his somewhere out there, fighting in the sand. He needed to get back outside. Fighting was his forte, and he was at his most effective when he wasn't cooped up inside.

He grabbed a short sword and stuck it in the sheath on his leg. He checked his weapons one last time and shook his head, muttering, "Sure wish I hadn't told Katie to stay in New York."

The intercom overhead crackled and squealed. It was Katie, and Calvin could hear the urgency in her voice. "Hold on tight. Pandora and I are on the way. ETA ten miles."

Calvin put his head back and laughed. "I should have known Katie wouldn't listen."

Calvin took the staircase up to the emergency hatch on

the surface, since at that point, none of the elevators were working. He slowly lifted the hatch, sticking his gun out first. He swiveled his weapon around the opening, making sure none of the demons were going to jump on it or him. He was lucky he had looked before he leaped. Three demons were standing just ten feet away with their backs to Calvin. He very slowly and quietly lifted the lid.

He rested his gun on the edge of the emergency hatch and pulled the trigger. Adjusted. Pulled the trigger again. The last demon was just turning around when Calvin's third shot separated his head from his body. The three demons became dust in the wind. "Guess you should've found another place to hang out."

Calvin grunted as he pulled himself out onto the platform, then stood up and dusted the sand off his pants. He pulled his bandanna up around his nose and mouth. The wind was wicked, and the last thing he needed was to choke on sand while trying to kill demons. The guys in the production building were still shooting, and in the killing field demons were still dying. The stream of demons had slowed down to a trickle, but they definitely weren't done.

One of the guys on the top of the building waved his arms at Calvin feverishly. Calvin stepped forward and squinted his eyes, following the guard's finger to the bottom of the building. Below the blast shields, a demon was trying to scratch his way through the cinderblock walls. "Oh hell, no."

Calvin walked forward and held the trigger of his weapon down, filling the demon with bullets. Calvin gave the guy up top a thumbs-up, and the guard returned it. The guard went back to taking out whatever came out of the portal. Before Calvin could get too far from the emergency hatch, it flung open. He leveled his weapon, his finger wrapping around the trigger.

Stephanie popped her head up, yelped, and put a hand in front of her face to make sure Calvin didn't blow it off.

Calvin lowered his weapon and helped Stephanie out of the hatch. Korbin and five guards followed her. They had obviously gone down to reload, since they were bristling with fresh weapons, ammo, and blades. Calvin stared thoughtfully at the seven of them and then at the demons. "Who else is there?"

One of the guards stepped forward and shook his head. "They got a whole lot of us. We were at the front gates, and they just kind of swarmed us from behind. Everyone else is inside the production building."

Calvin glanced briefly at Korbin and then at the portal. It began to spark and shimmer. "It looks like another wave of demons is coming. It also looks like it's just the eight of us, plus the guys up top. We have to hold on until she gets here."

Korbin nodded his head and pulled out his guns. "I think we can handle this. What do *you* think, dear?"

Stephanie gave Korbin a peck on the cheek and pulled her knives. "I think we can, and afterward, maybe I'll make one of those casseroles you like."

Calvin just gazed at the two of them and started to laugh. "I swear, it's like *Commando* meets *Leave It to Beaver*. One of these days I swear I'm going to see Stephanie rolling through a bunch of demons, blasting their heads off while wearing an apron."

Stephanie winked at Calvin. "Actually, Korbin's the one who usually wears the apron."

Calvin shook his head at Korbin. "We'll have to discuss that when this is all over."

Korbin watched Calvin walk away, and Stephanie patted him on the shoulder, laughing. Korbin yelled after him, "What? I don't like to get food on my pants."

They spread out and prepared themselves for the next round of battle. The trickle of demons became a monstrous flood as they began pouring through the portal again. They scrambled over one another and rushed to the killing field. Calvin, Korbin, and Stephanie were there to meet them. The other guards stayed behind to cover them and man the traps.

Even without a demon, Stephanie was ungodly fast and insanely agile. She went sprinting toward a line of demons, firing. When she met the line, she dropped and slid through the sand, gliding right between two scaly horrors. It reminded her of playing Red Rover as a child. She popped up behind the line and opened fire, and demons howled and exploded into ash. Red Rover had never ended quite like that.

Calvin stopped and stared at her with wide eyes. "That was some shit, right there."

Stephanie slammed another clip into her gun and smiled. "I told you I didn't need a demon. Just wait until I get warmed up."

Calvin laughed and leaped to his right, raising his gun and pulling the trigger without looking. A demon was lurching toward him, and the bullet went straight into the demon's head. It turned to dust in mid-air and blew away with the wind. Stephanie looked impressed.

Calvin shrugged nonchalantly. "I've been known to kick an ass or two myself."

The level of showmanship that Korbin and Stephanie brought to the table when they joined Calvin on the battlefield was impressive, but there was no way they could keep it up. The battle sucked. Hundreds of demons flooded the base, fighting with teeth and claws. There were only three mercs and five guards to fight them off. The guards on top of the production building did what they could, but they couldn't chance firing at the killing field and hitting their own men.

There were too many demons.

A huge rush of demons pushed the mercs back and made an opening, then scrambled past the guards to the production building. Calvin doubled back, spraying the demons with bullets as he ran to the base of the building.

"Whoa, back up you beady-eyed bastard," Calvin roared as he bent backward to avoid a demon's slashing claws.

He pulled a sword from his back one-handed and sliced the demon in half, and it snarled and spat even as it fell in two pieces to the ground and turned to dust. He chuckled and turned to continue the fight, but he felt the all-too-familiar sting of demon's claws across his back. The sword sheaths on his back were torn loose and his Kevlar was shredded, then came the hot-poker sear as talons ripped his flesh.

Calvin somersaulted forward and spun, slashing his sword down. The demon howled and retreated. Calvin had taken the thing's nose off. He raised his gun and pulled the trigger without thinking, blasting the demon four times in the chest. He shook his head and realized that it needed to be a headshot. He raised his weapon and pressed the trigger again, putting a bullet through the bleeding hole that used to be the demon's nose. His next shot took the demon's head off its shoulders. Calvin winced and looked over his shoulder at the blood running down his back. His black shirt was in tatters.

Calvin was definitely being tested. He had not faced this many demons at once in a very long time, and even then, he'd had Katie by his side. Korbin and Stephanie were making a dent, but the fighting was taking a toll on their human bodies. Stephanie had found that using her guns was the best she could do. Getting close to the demons was almost impossible without a demon of her own. She didn't remember what it was like to fight demons, but she had definitely overestimated her strength.

Korbin was having the same problem. He made his way to Stephanie, and together they backed out of the center of the fight and pulled back to the edges. "There's no use in getting yourself killed the first time out. It's obvious that without demons we aren't as strong, but that doesn't mean that we can't help. We'll lay down cover. Aim for the head."

Stephanie nodded. "That's one thing I've got over the demons. Sharpshooting is my specialty."

She took aim at a group of demons headed their way, let out a deep breath, and pressed the triggers over and over, slowly and surely. Each bullet found a demon, and each demon turned to dust. When Stephanie finally lowered her gun, Korbin was impressed. "Nice. I didn't know you could shoot like that."

Stephanie shrugged. "Honestly, I didn't either. It was just a gut feeling."

Korbin sighed. "Let's hope all your gut feelings turn out like this."

Stephanie giggled and continued firing at the horde. Korbin juked to the right as a group of demons tried to sneak up on them. He took two of them out before they attacked, then pulled his knife and used hand-to-hand combat techniques to avoid their claws. Stephanie shot three more demons and then raced over to help her husband. "You need to back off my man or you're gonna see my wrath."

Stephanie dodged a slashing claw and countered it with a roundhouse kick to the demon's face. Using her acrobatic skills, she crouched and then flipped over the stunned demon. She grabbed him by the head and twisted hard, breaking his neck. She smiled broadly and looked at Korbin. "See? Not that bad."

Korbin's eyes went big, and he pointed behind her. "Watch out!"

Stephanie turned to lash her foot out in another kick, but huge claws were already moving toward her. Hellish talons dug through her Kevlar, piercing her back and digging deep furrows in her skin all the way around her side. Stephanie threw a knife at the hulking demon, not seeing where it landed, then grabbed her open wounds and fell to the ground. Blood trickled into the sand. Korbin ran over to her and fired wildly, scattering demons. He helped her to her feet and saw the blood pooling beneath her. "Shit. It's bad."

"Just a scratch." Stephanie tilted her head up and grinned at him. "Hey, I gave it my best shot."

Korbin kissed her. "And you did a fucking fantastic job, but take your ass inside and get those tended to. You can't fight like that. Remember, you're only human. Use that aim, baby."

Stephanie held her bleeding side with one hand and fired with the other. Together they ran for the emergency hatch, shooting several demons in the process.

Korbin kissed her again and shut the lid behind her.

Korbin's face went grim, and he stalked back out to find whoever had done that to his wife. He found the hulking demon standing in the sand, trying to pull Stephanie's knife from his stomach. Her blood still coated his claws.

Korbin narrowed his eyes and pulled the sword from his back. "No one touches my wife."

The demon grinned, displaying rows of jagged teeth. He let go of the knife in his stomach and flicked out his boil-covered tongue to lick Stephanie's blood from his claws.

Korbin screamed and launched himself at the demon. He swung his sword two-handed and felt the brutal crunch as it bit into the demon's neck, but then he slammed to the ground and looked up. He had taken the demon's head right off. He wiped the demon's blood from his face but kept his eyes on the putrid head rolling across the sand until it turned to ash. Several of the other guards jogged up, patting him on the shoulder.

One of the guards was breathing heavily as he set the

butt of his gun in the sand. "I think this wave is about over. The guys up top, they got the rest of them. I lost one man, so we're down to seven."

Korbin shook his head. "Six. My wife took a wound across the back, so I sent her down into the bunker."

Timothy's voice came over their earpieces. "Guys, I hate to say this, but there is one big motherfucking demon coming out of that gate right now."

Korbin and the rest of the team looked at the portal. What was coming through it was as big as a house. His horned feet touched the ground, and the earth shook. Korbin growled, "Fuck me."

The thunderous landing of the emerging demon was drowned out by the whine of a squadron of fighter jets on the horizon.

Korbin put his hands on his knees, pushed out a deep puff of air, and let himself smile. "I thought they'd never get here. Damn military hasn't changed. Hurry up and wait."

The abomination stood up, and the guards gaped. He cracked his large neck and scanned the killing field. At once he was peppered with bullets. He snarled and looked toward the top of the production building, where the shots had come from. The guards quickly realized he didn't even have to tilt his head. He was so tall that he was eye-level with the top of the building.

The grizzled head guard swallowed hard. "All right, boys, he's just one big asshole. If we can kick a whole bunch of little assholes, we can kick one big one. We've only got one Damned merc down there and the rest are human, so we've got to give them as much backup as we possibly can. Take your places, and be ready for anything."

As the hulking mound of scale and claw lumbered toward the building, the squadron of jets soared over him and fired. The demon paused to watch as they made another pass.

Inside the gate, Moloch and Baal leaned forward excitedly. They laughed as the planes took runs at the massive demon.

Moloch pointed at the demon's confused face. "Did you see the look on the big one's face? That plane hit him with everything it had, and it was like somebody pinched him."

Baal laughed and slammed his scaled hand on the table. "We should do this more often! I love watching incursions. It's amazing how useless the humans are without the meat-sack and Lilith. They are absolutely clueless. They have no idea how to take down one of these bastards."

Moloch shrugged his shoulders. "They used to be inde-structible. Of course, technology has enhanced the humans, and the demons haven't changed. Things are a little different now. Still, it's absolutely hilarious to watch them shit their pants. They don't even know where to begin. I fucking love the big one."

Baal pointed at another plane diving at the demon. "Here comes another jet!"

The demon raised his arms in front of his face as though he were protecting itself and his twisted claws began to glow. Giant chunks of lava pulled directly from hell appeared on those huge claws, and he hurled them at the plane, laughing.

"Oh, shit!" the pilot yelled.

One of the boulders of molten lava soared through the air, but the pilot quickly rolled the plane away from it. He got lucky. The second pilot didn't. The other ball of lava hit the second jet's engine and sent the plane spinning out of control. The pilot panicked and pulled his seat ejection lever. He was launched from the plane as the rear end burst into flames.

The pilot's parachute opened and caught air, and wind took him away from the battle, drifting off somewhere in the mountains.

Calvin grimaced as the plane hit the ground and exploded into a giant ball of fire. The large demon was pelted with debris but didn't even seem to notice. He lurched forward, setting his sights on the prize. It was obvious that the demons were no longer testing them, but now sending out their big guns to get to the weapons.

Calvin grabbed Korbin with panic. "We've got to stop them!"

Korbin looked at his sword, wondering what use it would be against something the size of a building.

Another sound broke over the battle. Not the whine of a jet engine, but a deep, steady thunder of another, larger plane.

Baal and Moloch immediately stood up, recognizing that the sound was not that of another military plane. They stepped to the edge of the gate and peered off into the distance.

Baal slapped Moloch in the chest, as the plane got closer. "Do you think?"

Moloch shook his head. "She wouldn't be stupid enough to fly in on a private jet in the middle of a war zone. Probably some stupid government drone that was supposed to visit the base on a routine inspection and didn't realize they were in the middle of an incursion."

Baal screwed up his face and took a step back. "I don't

know, Moloch. Lilith has some crazy ideas. When you put her together with Katie, they seem to do the impossible."

Moloch kept his eyes on the plane. "Impossible yes. Stupid? No. They seem to be pretty smart when they're going into a battle situation. I wish it weren't so. I would love it if the bitch made that sort of deadly mistake. I'm not getting my hopes up, though. Besides, I want to keep her away as long as possible. We both know she can take down the big one, especially with whatever angelic power she's got."

The plane swerved and then began to slow as it dipped toward the runway. However, as soon as the wheels barely scraped the road it sped up again, lifting its nose into the air and taking back off. Moloch and Baal began to laugh.

Moloch slapped Baal in the stomach, forcing him to let out a huge puff of air. "That pilot just freaked the fuck out! He saw the big one and was like, 'Fuck this shit!'"

Baal straightened up and rubbed his stomach feeling the pain from Moloch's fist. "I know, right? He thought he was going to make a nice landing, and then all of a sudden, *bam*! There were demons everywhere. I don't think he was paying very good attention when he was coming in to land. It's not like you can miss a ten-story demon."

They continued to chuckle as they sat back down. Moloch shook his head with a smile on his face. "The fucking big one. Great stuff." He glanced out of the gate, and something caught his eye. He tilted his head to the right, and the smile began to fade. "What the hell?"

Baal stopped chuckling and looked out at the airstrip. "*It couldn't be*! She actually fucking did it!"

Strolling toward the base from the other side of the

landing pad was a lone body, strapped to the gills with weapons. She shook her hair out as the demons gawked at her from the portal.

Her wings popped open and Katie leaped into the air, flapping furiously as she climbed higher and began to do laps around the base.

Pandora chuckled. *I can almost feel the shock coming from inside that portal. Those two idiots Moloch and Baal must be watching the whole thing.*

Well, maybe they should've thought about this before they sent their demons to my house.

Pandora smirked. *I like it when you talk like that. I hope I get to see the shock on their faces when they lose this battle and we shove their demons right up their asses.*

Katie laughed wildly. *All there is to do now is show them exactly what we're made of. You don't come to my house uninvited, and you definitely don't bring all your idiot friends with you. I think it's time we taught them some manners.*

I couldn't agree more.

Calvin put his hands up and let out a whistle as Katie glided through the air. "I'm damn glad to see her."

Katie smiled at Calvin and nodded, continuing to fly around the base to scope out the entire battle. She hovered for a moment when the emergency hatch opened and Stephanie climbed out. She had white bandages around her back and side. Blood was spotting the white, but she cradled a weapon in her arms. She hobbled over next to Korbin, who gave her an arm to lean on.

Katie and Pandora raged. Pandora could not believe Stephanie was that gravely injured and still on the field. *Oh, hell, no! Somebody went after my baby girl!*

Katie scanned the rest of the base. *Not to mention all the damage they've done to my house. It's gonna take a lot of money and time to repair this shit. These motherfuckers came to the wrong place.*

Katie's eyes glowed red as she swooped closer to the production building to make sure the shield was still in place and everything was secure. The grizzled guard on the roof gave her a sloppy salute as she passed. It seemed as though the guards up top had done a pretty damn good job of keeping the demons out. She flew around the building, satisfied.

She stopped when she saw a fresh group of demons pour out of the portal. They were small demons; lesser ones that she would love to pick up and snap in half. Not the time. She had vengeance in her heart.

Down on the ground, Calvin could see the next wave of demons emerging. "All right, guys, here they come again. We can't leave it all up to Katie, so let's give her the best backup we can."

Stephanie was ready to go and checked her gun. Korbin pushed the barrel down. "What do you think you're doing?"

Stephanie shrugged. "I never let a few scratches get to me before."

Korbin lifted an eyebrow at her. "By a few scratches, you mean from the rose bushes back at home? Not from demon claws. Trust me, there'll be more fights. Go down and get healed for now. And stay there."

Stephanie studied him intently and snarled, "Are you telling me what to do?"

Korbin spoke softly but put his foot down. "I am. This time, I am."

Slowly a smile moved over Stephanie's lips, and she leaned up and kissed him. "Don't make it a habit, but I have to say…it's kind of sexy."

Calvin walked up to the two of them. They were battered and bloody and still looked like a couple of dogs in heat. He cleared his throat. "Uh, we ready?"

Stephanie nodded and slapped Korbin's shoulder. "I'm going to sit this one out, but good luck."

Katie pumped her wings hard and flew up high, then hovered over the battlefield. The sun streamed over her shoulders and trickled over the desert. From below, all they could see was the shadow of Katie's giant wings spread wide. Katie took a deep breath, and her body emitted a blinding stream of light. She tipped forward and folded her wings back, diving as fast as she could toward the battlefield, and right at the gigantic demon who was lumbering toward the production building.

She pulled out her angelic sword and held it high over her head as she slammed into the demon. In a fluid motion, she drove her angelic sword into the back of his head and through his skull. She held on tightly as the creature flailed, growling loudly and whimpering. He was layer upon layer of infernal muscle, and he couldn't get his huge arms around his bulk. He waved his claws behind him, but couldn't reach high enough to knock her off. His claws began to glow, pulling great boulders of molten rock from hell.

Katie levered her angelic sword back and forth and the demon began to waver.

"That's right, buddy, just give in to it. You can go right back down to hell and have yourself a nice little cocktail on me," Katie whispered to the demon.

The demon's eyes rolled back in its head, and it fell. Katie held on tightly and pulled the sword from the beast's skull and rode it all the way down, and the earth shook as it landed. One moment Katie stood on its head, a conquering hero, and the next, the demon burst into a cloud of ash that hid Katie from sight. The wind picked up, and the ash swirled and began to blow toward the mountains. From a distance, the guards saw Katie walking through the dissipating ash, fully armored and holding her sword tightly. Two cooling mounds of lava were all that remained of the big one.

Korbin sliced the top of a demon's head off as he watched Katie emerge from the ash. He yelled at Calvin, "The girl sure knows how to make an entrance."

Calvin chuckled, then stabbed a demon in the throat with a dagger and finished it with a gunshot to the head. "You have no idea, buddy. I blame that on Pandora. She's the one with the flair for dramatics."

One of the guards on top of the production building whistled. "Too bad the movie cameras aren't here, because this girl would blow Wonder Woman out of the water."

The grizzled guard shrugged. "I mean, get her a whip, and I'm sold."

As Katie strutted across the sand, Pandora gave her a play-by-play of the reactions of the people in the area.

Maybe this angelic armor isn't as bad as I thought. I do need to see this Wonder Woman, though. She's come up several times.

Katie laughed and pulled a gun from her holster. *That's definitely one I can get down with.*

I'm just interested in the whip part.

All across the base the guards were locking and loading, getting ready to rush in to support Katie. Joshua raised the shield on the front doors and holstered his guns on his chest. In his hands he now held two large axes, the special metal shimmering in the sunlight. He was no longer the meek kid Katie had met so long ago. He was a grown man, and he was going to stand up for his home and back up his demonic boss.

Katie gave Joshua a nod of approval. She wasn't keen on him fighting, but she knew she couldn't stop him. Despite herself, she was pretty proud of him for what he had become.

Pandora cleared her throat. *So, are we going to annihilate this wave of bastard demons, or what?*

Hey, give me a fucking second. I just took down a giant demon in my first three seconds on the ground, and I used my angelic powers to do it.

Pandora scoffed. *Oh, I didn't realize this was a competition. If that's the case, then settle in, bitch. These demons are going down.*

Katie smirked. She had gotten the reaction she wanted from Pandora. She gripped her magic sword in one hand and a gun in the other. She crouched and waited for Pandora to give her a burst of speed. Her wings had disappeared, but that was okay. Now that she was on the ground, she was all demon.

Pandora cackled loudly, giving her a burst of speed. *Hold on, sweet tits, we're going in for the kill!*

An explosion of energy erupted behind Katie, swirling the sand up as she took off across the field and barreled straight into the first wave of demons. She put her head down, raised her gun, and swung her angelic sword, cutting through them as though they were paper.

Calvin and the others watched the wave of energy she brought with her in amazement. It blew back at least half of the demons and sent them rolling across the desert.

Calvin scratched his head. "Looks like we have a super-hero on our hands."

The entire melee was absolutely horrible. There were demons, mercs, and humans all over the place. It was obvious that the smaller demons had no control or understanding of where they were supposed to be going. It was essentially a giant shit show.

The bullets from both those on the ground and those still shooting from the production building sprayed, heavily concentrated on the areas in front of Katie. It was backup, or maybe cover—anything to keep Katie on the go before all the demons could swarm her. There were so many that regardless of her powers and might, she was barely making a dent. After her first charge it was all defensive, trying to keep them away from the production building. When one was killed, another dozen emerged from the portal.

Fuck this! Katie snarled angrily.

These motherfuckers pulled all the demons out for this one. They are using the idiots from the far reaches of hell, Pandora replied, still giving Katie as much juice as she could.

I don't want to defend, I want to put a god damned stop to this mess. Where the fuck are those two idiots, Moloch and Fucknuts?

Pandora laughed out loud. They were probably lounging back in hell, snacking on some poor unfortunate creature. *My best guess is safely behind that portal.*

Katie slashed her sword, taking the heads off four demons who had made it through the gunfire from above. *They think they are safe in that portal, but I just might have different news for them.*

Uh... I don't know if you understand how the portal works?

Katie quickly pulled one of her pistols, firing at two demons leaping toward her. She struck them each in the head, and they grimaced and squirmed before turning to dust. She wiped her forehead with the back of her hand and let out a deep sigh. *I do know this: there are more demons here than our base can handle, and I only have two people with me who are Damned. The rest are humans, and there's no way I'm going to let Korbin and Stephanie die in this. I just brought them back, for fuck's sake!*

Pandora sensed a demon approaching. *To your left!*

Katie went low as the demon soared toward her, claws out and his teeth covered in blood from some poor victim. She shook her head and nonchalantly aimed, looking at the portal as she pulled the trigger. The bullet went straight through the demon's head, but Katie didn't even stop to watch it turn to dust. *This shit is stupid. This will keep going unless the source is taken out.*

Pandora grimaced. *I don't think you're quite ready for Lucifer.*

The demon on the ground squirmed and screeched so

Katie, eyes still focused on the gates, pointed her weapon down and shot it twice, turning it to dust. *You said it wasn't Lucifer, per se. And even if it is, if that's what needs to happen? So be it.*

Pandora sighed at Katie's stubbornness. Katie moved forward, slashing through the droves of demons. She was headed straight for the gate with anger in her red eyes. The demons slashed and gnarled, trying to overcome her. Several times she let out smaller pulses of energy, pushing back the front lines and then diving in to rip demons apart with her bare hands.

She stood up and stepped over a pile of demons as they turned to dust at her feet. She wiped the blood from her cheek. It was black and sticky, and she could barely get her hand away from her face. *What the fuck are your people made of? Tar?*

Pandora giggled. *More like souls, puppy dog innards, and angst.*

So, like a teenage boy?

Pandora watched as Katie grabbed a demon by the throat and pulled his head from his shoulders. Black blood splashed the sand. *Yeah, actually, pretty close,* Pandora admitted.

Not far away, Moloch and Baal watched as Katie rampaged through the lines of demons, giving zero fucks. Moloch gritted his teeth, pissed. He stood up, knocking his chair to the floor. He stomped to the edge of the gate and stared with bright red eyes at Katie. She tore a demon in half and seemed to stare right back, even though he knew she couldn't see him through the portal.

"This bitch has gone too far this time," he bellowed.

Baal wiped his hands on his black scaly legs and stood up with a grunt. He could see that Moloch was at the end of his rope. He picked up Moloch's chair, set it right, and stepped around the table. "Calm down Moloch, we knew she would kick the shit out of those lesser demons."

He looked at Baal with his hands out. "She killed the big one with a single jab of her fucking shimmering sword!"

Baal shrugged his shoulders. "So, send her a few more big ones. Let's see how she does with them."

Moloch's frustration faded, and an evil smile curled his lips. "You are a genius. If she thought one was easy, let's see how well she does with three."

Moloch waved his arms, sending a cloud of dark mist through the gate. When the mist touched the soil of Earth, it congealed, twisted, and solidified into three very large demons. Moloch smiled, and Katie stopped dead in her tracks.

He started to laugh. "What's wrong, bitch? Too much demon for you to handle?"

And then she leaped. Not at the three new big ones, but at the portal itself. At Moloch and Baal. Her eyes glowed bright blue from the angel inside her, and the wave of energy hit Moloch hard. He stumbled backward. Baal's eyes opened wide, and he scurried back. "Come on, let's get out of here."

Moloch nodded his head heavily. "We have to close the gate. Those on the other side can find their way back with a bullet to the head."

Moloch and Baal stood at the gate with their hands up, trying to close it. The harder they tried, the more it stuck. Both of them grunted loudly and pulled their arms open, but as soon as they released, the gate snapped back open.

"What the?" Baal panicked.

Moloch stared at Katie for a moment. She had turned back to the big ones. He watched the angel in her fighting the demons and realized what was happening. "I've never seen it done, but they are acting separately."

Baal looked at him confused. "What?"

Moloch narrowed his eyes. "Lilith is keeping the gate open while Katie is using her angelic powers to fight. Those bitches have figured out the duality of their powers."

Baal shook his head. "No one has ever been able to do that, not even when Lucifer went above and took over a body. One is always fully in charge."

"It seems that we are seeing something completely different this time," Moloch shouted.

He was livid, watching Katie jab her sword into one of the gigantic demon's heads and ride him to the ground like a badly-formed bull. Moloch glared at her even as he felt her angelic stare piercing his chest. She had her eyes locked on him, but he didn't think she could see through the portal. He *knew* she couldn't.

Both Moloch and Baal backed up again, moving around the table and standing as if it would provide some sort of protection. They watched as Katie attempted to kill the other two demons, her eyes locked on the portal. She wasn't going to give up, and she definitely wasn't going to let them think she was afraid.

Do they think sending a couple of oversized puffball demons will scare me off? Katie slashed through several smaller demons, spraying blood and dust everywhere.

That's what it looks like. I don't think they fully understand your abilities just yet.

Moloch and Baal continued to step back as Katie moved closer to the gate. Baal shook his head and looked at Moloch. "What is that bitch thinking? What's she going to do, invade hell?"

Moloch gave him a non-reassuring look and watched the battle ensue. He couldn't remember a time when a human had tried to invade hell, at least not one where they had survived. Then again, every time Katie and Pandora did something they shocked the hell out of him. The word "impossible" didn't seem to apply to the two of them.

"Whatever she is planning, I'm not even remotely considering watching it from the front lines," Baal whined.

Moloch stared out at Katie, watching the way she moved. "Agreed, but I *am* curious as to what is driving the human. Is it her angelic abilities? Is it Lilith? I have seen a lot of mercs in my time in hell, and I have battled a few as well. She is different. I give T'Chezz a bad rap, but he was a tough sonofabitch, and she took him down even before the angel powers became so prominent. She is definitely a force to be reckoned with."

On the other side of the world, waves gently crawled up the beach. The ocean had been calm all morning. The Mediterranean was seeing one of its more beautiful, bright blue days. The beaches were full of tourists and locals, all of them taking in the sun and sand, but around mid-day all that changed.

"Look, mommy, the waves! They're getting so big." The little boy marveled at the tide with his hands cupped around an elaborate sandcastle.

His mother glanced up with a smile, but her face quickly changed as she watched large waves begin to roll up onto the shore. She stood up from her chair and stepped forward, frowning out across the ocean. Just beyond a sandbar, large bubbles were rising to the surface. Water roiled all around it.

Several other beachgoers stopped what they were doing and joined the woman looking out over the ocean. "What in the world is that?"

Another sunbather replied, "I don't know. Maybe some sort of environmental thing?"

They stood there covered in suntan oil, in bathing suits and wide-brimmed sun hats. They sat in their beach chairs and under their umbrellas, with no idea of the terror that was about to rain down on that small Mediterranean beach. The bubbles grew larger and larger until it looked as if the ocean were boiling. The little boy put down his shovel and left his sandcastle. He walked over to the edge of the waves, tilting his head to the side. He suddenly grinned.

"A dinosaur!" the little boy yelled.

The mother's eyes grew wide and she ran for her son, grabbing her little boy around the waist and running down the beach. A Leviathan rose from the waves, the water sluicing off it in a cascade. People began screaming and running, never having seen anything like that before. The beast moved fast for its size and made its way to the shore within seconds.

His green, algae-covered skin shimmered in the sunlight as he beat his hands against his chest and roared loudly. The sound of his voice echoed across the small town, shaking the ground and breaking storefront windows. He stepped forward, crushing the little boy's sandcastle. The Leviathan raged as he descended upon the small beach town with all the anger of hell in his eyes.

He grabbed a small surfing shanty and picked it up high in the air, a surfer still inside. The twenty-something blond guy stared fearfully out the window as the beast raised the shanty high above his head. With a quick movement, the Leviathan threw it hard at the ground, smashing it and everything inside it. The blond surfer, bruised and bloody, tried to crawl from the wreckage, and the Leviathan stepped on him.

The beast grabbed a woman standing frozen in fear and ripped her head off with his jagged teeth. He tossed the woman's lifeless body to the ground, crunching on her skull like it was a kernel of popcorn. The Leviathan continued moving, crushing buildings and people every-where he looked. He moved fast and with a purpose, and that purpose was destruction. He flattened anything and anyone in his path.

"Where's the military? Where is help?" One of the tourists screamed out as several bodies rolled past her in the street.

The man standing next to her shook his head. "He looks like Godzilla. What could we do against Godzilla?"

The beast smashed across the beach, waving his deadly green claws around, and crashed through several of the resorts that sat on the shore. The tourists didn't even have a chance to evacuate. All were crushed either by his uncaring footfalls or the buildings he toppled onto them. On the streets of the small Mediterranean beach town, debris and bodies were strewn. Just moments before the place had been peaceful and beautiful, with fountains and merchants in the streets. Now it was a wasteland of screaming injured and wrecked lives.

The tactic had been hit-and-run, causing as much damage as possible in the shortest amount of time, and then retreating. Those who were left standing in the rubble watched as the large beast turned back toward the shore and stomped through the sand. He quickly submerged himself, disappearing back into the ocean. He roared wildly as his head sank beneath the sea's surface, and the waves quieted.

Staring at the calm sea, it was almost as if it had never happened. However, when you turned back around to look at the town, it looked as if a hurricane and a tornado had hit the town all at once. But the skies were blue, and the gentle breeze continued to flow, carrying the sounds of screaming humans out over the Mediterranean Sea.

One of the survivors wiped some blood from his cheek and shook his head. "What was the point of that? He came, destroyed, and was gone within fifteen minutes… So many people are dead!"

A military convoy pulled into the town and stopped short. The commander got out and took his hat off, shocked at the demolition before him. There was barely anything recognizable left of the town. The few survivors who were left were attempting to move the bodies of their friends and loved ones out of the streets. The attack had happened so quickly that the only emergency personnel who had been available to help were the local police, and from the looks of it, they were all dead now.

The commander stepped forward and frowned. "What in the world happened here? We got the call just twenty minutes ago."

A woman holding her child to her chest hobbled up to the commander and peered at him through tear-laden eyes. "It was a beast. I've never seen anything like him before. He hasn't been on the news stations or at any incursions. He came from the sea in a silence that was deafening. He ravaged the town and ripped people limb from limb and destroyed every building, and when he was done, he just walked back into the ocean and disappeared."

The commander stared at her for a moment and then looked out at the ocean with an eerie feeling.

14

Pandora was mad as hell. *Those fat fucktardian fopwits better have a moment to speak with my fucking fist!*

Katie grunted and sent a group of demons flying with a swing of her fist. *Don't worry, if they don't want to make room in their schedule for us, we'll just pop in unexpectedly. They can't possibly think they can send this kind of chaos to our doorstep and not expect some right back!*

Katie was hitting harder than she ever had before, unsure if it was a result of her powers or her armor. Demons flew with every punch, some of them even turning to ash as soon as the blows hit their skulls. She had a rage inside her that just wasn't going away. Every time she looked at the base and at her friends, it grew stronger.

Pandora watched as a smaller demon flew straight up into the air and hovered there for a second, and Katie slashed it in half. *I've never seen you fight like this before.*

That's because I've never fought like this before. I don't know, it's like I'm stronger than ever. Maybe it's the fact that I haven't eaten any donuts in a long time.

Pandora hissed. *Hey, don't go jumping to any conclusions. Donuts are in our future, trust me. For them not to be, you would have to bring me some serious scientific evidence that they inhibit your fighting ability. Even then, we might just have to take one for the team.*

We? You mean I would have to take one for the team. We are the team.

Pandora held strong. *I'm telling you, some serious scientific evidence would have to be presented. You don't just walk into a girl's house and tell her she can't have donuts.*

Katie snickered at the comment. Her angelic sword disappeared, and she pulled out both of her pistols and began shooting. Demons howled in pain and exploded into ash. The two larger ones were stomping around, seemingly lost in the sea of hellish beings. They had their eyes on the production building, but there was no fucking way Katie was going to let them anywhere near it. In fact, she was tired of their antics, and ready to send them straight back to hell.

"Hey," Katie yelled to one of the them. That grabbed its attention.

She put her pistols away and cleared her throat, standing up straight in her armor. "Yeah, you. I'm talking to you. Why don't you come over here and let me kick your motherfucking balls off?"

The demon smirked and growled. It turned toward her, taking the bait. She shook her head and giggled to herself. The demon seemed to be stupider than she actually thought possible.

A small demon came running straight for Katie, and she reared back and punched it as hard as she could. The blow stopped the little guy in his tracks. It stood there for a second, wobbling back and forth. Katie laughed.

I think I knocked the hell right out of this one.

I've never seen eyeballs roll like that before, at least not in something's head.

Katie reached out with one finger and pushed and the demon fell backward, turning to ash before it hit the ground. She put her fist in front of her face and grinned maliciously. She had a whole new weapon, and this one was attached to her body. She nodded in approval and looked at the large demon walking toward her.

"Oh, good, you take orders well," Katie taunted the beast as she rubbed her hands together.

Katie dug her heels in and ran straight for the demon. She didn't really have a plan, figuring she would just go with the flow. As she grew closer to it, she jumped up, skipping across the heads of some of the smaller demons, and leaped on the large one, grabbing the monster near its waist. The beast stopped, confused. It shifted right and left, trying to see Katie over its immense scaly belly.

Pandora yawned. *Nothing like a little rock climbing to keep your body fit and firm.*

Katie grunted as she climbed the demon, making her way up to its shoulder. She looked at the other mountainous demon stalking toward them, bright red eyes shining. She clapped her hands together and rubbed them furiously. She took a step back, then leaped off the demon's shoulder. She stretched her arms out as she flew, not even needing her wings to make it over to the other demon. She grabbed the sides of the demon's head and in a smooth motion, she threw her body around, swung through the air, taking the horrible head with her and breaking the demon's neck.

The demon let out a strange, childish gurgle and fell. Katie swung onto the back of its neck and stood firm as it hit, shaking the ground. Katie hopped off the dead demon and covered her face as it burst into a cloud of ash.

Three down, one to go, Katie boasted.

I'm just over here imagining you doing that to its balls. You make a running leap, grab onto its nutsack, and swing around. You could bring any demon to its knees. Any angel too, probably.

Katie shrugged as she walked toward the other demon. The big guy must have heard the nutsack discussion because he made a break for the portal. *Meh, seems like a lot of work just to climb up and kill it. Besides, I really don't want to hug a giant demon's balls.*

Good point. It's pretty damn hot in hell, and I can only imagine the sweat on those things.

Katie grimaced, feeling her stomach turn. *God, it would be like a demon fucking Slip-and-Slide. So gross.*

Portals usually closed whenever the mercs were winning, but this time it stayed open. Even the dumbest of the small demons couldn't help but notice, and some ran back through. They could see they had been outdone, especially with Katie there. Making a run for it was the only thing they knew to do.

I don't know whether to chase them or just let them go, Katie complained. She put her hands on her hips and watched the retreating horde.

I would conserve the energy. Besides, they'll just end up back in hell, to be turned around and sent right back here. If they're making a run for it, it's like a win for you. You don't have to spend your time ripping their heads off.

Katie chuckled. *But I like it. Gets out some of my aggression.*

I know something else that would help get your aggression out.

My sex life should not be a topic of conversation right now.

Pandora giggled. *Just saying. Just saying.*

Katie clapped her hands together and looked at their people standing close to the production building. *Okay, I need you to give me two excellent demons to support our humans. No wimpy bitch demons or drama-starting fools, just big bad brawling demons who will listen when we tell them to do something.*

Actually, two of them just ran back into hell. I knew them from my days sitting lazily next to Lucifer on the throne.

Katie smirked. *I need them to be willing to help us. I don't need them to be loyal, just willing to take instruction—which means they can't be Lucifer's lackeys.*

Oh, trust me, their loyalties lie with whoever will keep them safe. One word from me and they will be eating out of your hands, or the hands of whoever you stick them in.

That was exactly what I wanted to hear. Katie beamed, then rolled her shoulders and cracked her neck, readying herself.

Katie stepped back, dug her feet into the ground, and made sure her armor was on securely. She stared nervously at the portal, not looking forward to what she was about to do. She couldn't put this off. She had seen the vulnerabilities in her team, and there was no way she was going to let them perish just because they weren't Damned. They deserved the right to have a chance to make a difference in this war.

Katie took off running toward the portal and Pandora began to get nervous. *Hold up! What the fuck are you doing? Are you a total fucking moron? Shit. I'm stuck in this human who's now running straight for hell! Well, I guess I don't have much say, so fuck it! Let's do this!*

"So, in total four large demons came through the portal. Katie took down three of those, and the other ran back into the portal when the fight slowed down," one of the pilots explained, getting the general up to speed.

"Good. And where are we now?"

The pilot cleared his throat nervously. "Well, the last of the small demons are jumping back through the portal. The building's guards seem to be cleaning up, picking off any of the smaller demons who got left behind."

The general lifted an eyebrow, noticing he didn't say anything about Katie. "And Katie?"

The pilot was silent for a moment. "I'll be honest; I'm not really sure. With all the ruckus I kind of lost track of her, but just a moment ago she was making a run straight for the gate."

The general slapped his hand on the desk. "What? Did you just say she was running *for the gate to hell?*"

The pilot stuttered. "Y-yes Sir. I'm not exactly sure what she was planning."

The general leaned back in his chair and shook his

head. "I don't think anybody knows what that girl is planning until it comes to fruition."

The general looked up as his secretary poked her head in the door. "You have a call from one of the higher-ups. You might want to take this."

The general nodded and turned back to his conversation. "Well, keep me updated on what's going on there. If you need any more help, let me know and I'll send some. And for God's sake, when Katie gets back from doing whatever the hell it is she is doing, please have her give me a call."

The general hung up and took a deep breath, getting his nerves together before answering the other call. "This is General Brushwood."

"General, I'm sorry to bother you. I know you're dealing with an incursion in Nevada, but I think you're going to want to see this." The chief of staff was breathless. He continued, "There was a huge issue in a small beach town in the Mediterranean. We are sending the footage to you via ComSat 331."

That caught the general's attention. "Of course, Sir. Give me one minute to get the satellite pulled up."

The general put the chief of staff on hold, clicked the line over, and dialed his IT department. "This is the general. I need you to pull video from ComSat 331 on channel thirty-three, security code given. Push that over to my office screen, please."

The IT guy agreed, and the general switched back over to the chief of staff as the picture began to appear in front of him. "Okay, sir, the video's coming up. What exactly am I looking… Holy hell! What is that?"

Both the general and the chief of staff watched in shock as they viewed the last part of the Mediterranean town's destruction by the Leviathan. It was a satellite view, but they could still see the buildings burning and people running through the streets. It was reminiscent of a war-torn area where bombs had gone off, but from the looks of it, what the creature had done was much worse.

The general was stunned. Onscreen, the beast walked back into the ocean. Neither man spoke a word until the beast was completely submerged and the ocean was calm again. The chief of staff cleared his throat. "As you can see, we have a bit of an issue."

The general shook his head, gathering his wits. "Do we know where it went?"

The chief of Staff was silent for a moment. "Not really. It came up without warning or detection. It ravaged the town, and the military showed up just as it was sinking back into the ocean. The survivors were able to point out where it went down, and some of ours and our allies' submarines were able to track it for a little while, but then it just disappeared. We don't know if it went through a portal or if it's hiding somewhere down there."

The general clicked on his computer and glanced at the data for that time period. "I don't see anything on here showing any kind of portal activity in the area. Then again, I'm not sure one would even show up that deep in the ocean."

"Those were my thoughts, but the subs couldn't track it. It was like the whole damn thing just disappeared. How does a beast the size of Godzilla just vanish?" The chief of staff was irritated, but not at the general.

The general shook his head. "I don't know, sir. What I can do is get this footage to some of my experts, and we can figure things out. If we are capable of detecting portals before they even appear, we should be able to figure out where this monster disappeared to. I don't know what kind of intelligence it has, but from the looks of it, and from the amount of time it spent in the town, it had a specific task."

"I agree. From some of the testimony coming in from the survivors, everything happened within fifteen minutes. It was a damn hit-and-run, and nobody had a chance to even take cover. All those women and children!" The chief of staff's voice caught in his throat.

The general couldn't believe what was going on. There had been two large hits in one day, and neither of them could be fully explained. "Let me get on this. I'll let you know what I find out as soon as I get the information. We'll find this monstrosity, sir. That's what we're best at."

15

Knowing that insane ventures should be undertaken quickly, Katie leaped through the portal. She landed on one knee on hot rock and sat there for a second with her head down, feeling the incredible energy raging around her. It pulled at her and pushed at her. She could feel it almost as if her body were absorbing those energies into her bloodstream. It was incredibly intense, and she wasn't prepared for it.

Slowly she lifted her head and put her hand on her knee, pushing herself to her feet. The angelic sword appeared in her hand again, and she sheathed it at her waist. The energy was so strong she could see it swirling through the portal. The area was dark, only small rays of light in the background leading into the large pits of hell. The heat was exhausting and threatened to melt the clothes right off her body.

Shit, and you lived in this? It's like one of those scenes in horror movies where the girl gets stuck in the sauna, and it's turned all the way up. I feel like it could melt the skin right off my face.

Pandora chuckled. *You see now why the Nevada heat didn't really bother me? It's not that bad once you get down to the bottom. It kind of disperses. But this is a tunnel straight into hell, so you really feel it here. Don't worry, I'll make sure your skin is still intact when we get out. I would suggest hurrying and doing whatever it is you need to do so your angel wings don't melt right off.*

Katie chuckled. *For some reason, I think that the angel wings would be the things that lasted the longest in this heat. I feel like they are probably time-tested and hell-approved.*

I don't think I want to find out, and I've never seen an angel in hell before. At least not one who's not fallen.

Katie rubbed her eyes, trying to clear her vision and get a better view of what was going on around her. *I guess there's a first time for everything. I'm not full angel, though, so I don't know if it'll count.*

Do they have a record book for those things?

If they don't, I'm definitely making one.

Pandora concentrated part of her energy on keeping Katie's body safe while scanning the area for the demons she wanted to recruit, and for any further sign of Moloch. That was one demon she wouldn't be even remotely sad to face. She had fantasized about his overly large head rolling across Times Square just like T'Chezz's had. She'd kick it all the way across that town and into the fields on the outskirts. It was a beautiful thing for Pandora to envision, since she hated those idiots so much.

Pandora took control of Katie's arm and pointed her

finger straight at two demons. *There they are! Those are the two idiots I was talking about.*

Katie narrowed her eyes and stared at the two demons. They were having some sort of argument, one bitching at the other. The second demon patted the first on the shoulder reassuringly. "It's fine. Stop being such a pussy. We got through the portal, and she's not going to bring her flammable meatsack over here into the heat."

The first demon narrowed his eyes at him suspiciously. "She's not exactly a regular human."

The other one scoffed. "Come on, even angels don't venture down here."

His companion's eyes got huge, and he followed his line of sight and shrieked. Running as fast as she could through the gates of hell was Katie, adorned in her angel armor and carrying her bright white sword. Before they could move, Katie was on them. She grabbed them both by the neck and lifted them into the air. "You two are coming with me."

Both demons were too scared to say a word and just hung there, staring at her. She began to make her way back out of the portal, but demons were everywhere. They were starting to notice that there was an angel among them. Several of the smaller demons lurched toward her, ready to attack and save the others. She rolled her eyes and shook her head. "Can't anything be easy?"

The two knucklehead demons looked at her and smirked, but she wasn't giving up that easily. She pulled her arms apart, dangling them above ground, and then smashed them together. Their heads collided with a sharp crack, knocking both out. She nodded, satisfied, and tossed one over each shoulder, then awkwardly drew her sword.

She studied the demons attacking and shrugged. "You had the chance to get away. I wasn't going to mess with you, but here you are, trying to attack me. I guess I'm gonna have to put this sword through your faces. And I'm pretty sure that if I kill you here, you don't come back."

Katie swung her sword, taking off the heads of the demons before they could even move. The demons slung over her shoulders restricted her movement, but she didn't mind. She grinned and slashed. Instead of turning to ash like they did on Earth, the demons screamed and exploded into black mist that floated into the portal. Katie was surprised for a moment; she was not expecting that. She shrugged, figuring it was a lot cleaner than the dust she always had to clean off her shoes.

Only a few other demons tried to attack her, but Katie was on a roll. She figured if she was there, she might as well take as many as she could. If killing them ended their lives here in hell, she could cut down on Moloch's army. Even a small reduction in his demonic forces would be positive.

Pandora scoffed. *Like there aren't plenty of human souls to be sent down here at a moment's notice.*

Yeah, well, I didn't really think about that. Plus, it's kind of fun to watch them explode. It's like squeezing a grape. Pop!

Pandora scanned the area around them. *Gig's up! Lots coming! We've gotta go!*

Katie pouted but sheathed her sword, then flipped the demons off her shoulders and held them by their necks as she took off at a run. The demons were flooding through the gate, trying to get back into hell before it closed. It was like driving down a one-way street in the wrong direction during rush hour in New York City, only she was carrying two bodies.

Katie shook her head and backed up. She couldn't fight through that kind of crowd, especially not with two demons clutched in her fists. She took off at a run and jumped high, her wings sprouting from her back, and she soared over the horde of demons and out of the portal. As soon as she was through, a rush of cool air hit her in the face. She let out a deep breath and drew in air untainted by sulfur and the damned. She sighed as she touched down on the ground. Her wings folded up and disappeared.

Calvin let out a relieved sigh as soon as he saw Katie. "That girl is going to give me a heart attack. Everybody thinks I'm gonna die from a demon incursion, but it's going to be worrying about Katie and her crazy antics that does me in."

Korbin tilted his head to the right. "What the hell is she carrying?"

Calvin squinted and took a step forward. "What the fuck? She's got two unconscious demons in her hands. What the hell is she gonna do with those?"

Everyone, including the human guards, was shocked to see Katie carrying out two comatose demon bodies. Katie had done a lot of weird things in the name of winning a war, but diving into hell and coming back with demons was a new one. She slowly walked toward the guards, just glad she was no longer burning to death in hell.

Pandora cackled at everyone's shock. *I think you surprised them for once. I'm pretty sure they thought they had gotten to the point where nothing you did could surprise them.*

Katie gave a crooked smile. *I guess I gotta keep them on*

their toes. By the way, thanks for keeping that portal open. I'm not exactly sure what I would've done if it had closed while I was in there.

The air crackled with electricity and thunder boomed overhead. The sky over the base shimmered, and a crackle echoed across the killing field. The portal had snapped shut. Pandora was silent for a second, and then cleared her throat. *Uh, as much as I like to take responsibility for the good things, I had nothing to do with keeping the portal open. I actually thought it was you.*

Nope. At least, I don't think so.

Katie walked up to Korbin and Calvin, who grimaced at the demons she was clutching. She looked over her shoulder at the guards, who were kicking at loose hunks of concrete the demons had torn from the base of the production building. It would take a lot of work to repair.

Joshua picked up a stone and tossed it into a pile. "At least it's not as bad as last time."

Katie tilted her head and grunted. "Calvin, Korbin, and Timothy? Before you guys get started on the base thing, I want you guys to come with me underground. Where's Stephanie?"

Korbin seemed nervous. "She's down there. Originally, they had just bandaged her up, but she needed stitches. One of the girls is a nurse, and she's taking care of her."

"Good. Come on, let's go down there," Katie ordered. "We will grab her on the way." Katie shook the demons, and they woke up, hissing and struggling.

Timothy pulled out his tablet and started pressing buttons, and all the lights and electricity came back on.

Korbin looked at him, impressed. "You can do all that from a tablet?"

Timothy put his arm around Korbin as they walked toward the elevator. "I could rule the world from this tablet."

Korbin raised an eyebrow. "I'm not sure if that's a good thing."

Katie struggled to drag the two demons across the sand. They were acting up, but she didn't want to knock them out again. "I'll take the emergency hatch with these two idiots. I'll meet you down there."

When Katie approached the emergency hatch and flung it open, the demons tried to avoid going down into the base. "Stop struggling, or I'll knock you the fuck out again."

Pandora cleared her throat and sat up straight inside of Katie. *Let me take care of this. Hey, you two fucking idiots. Don't you understand that you've been caught by not only the famous mercenary Katie, but Lucifer's wife? That's me. You need to settle the fuck down before I get involved.*

One of the demons growled. *I don't have to listen to you. You're weak. Powerless. Lucifer is even talking about taking a new wife. That makes you just another lonely demon on Earth.*

Pandora cackled. *Is that what you really think? I can show you just how powerless I really am. And I promise you, afterward you're going to have to clean off the shit and piss.*

Katie smiled as the two demons calmed down and went silent. She tossed the beasts down and jumped into the hatch after them, then dragged them down the hall, stopping at the sickbay.

Stephanie was laid out on one of the stretchers. She was gritting her teeth and holding onto the edge of the stretcher as the nurse finished her stitches and put on fresh bandages. She let out a deep breath and sat up slowly. She dangled her legs over the edge but put on a brave face when she saw Katie

Katie gave her a sympathetic look. "You okay?"

Stephanie patted her bandages with a wince. "I am now. Stitches suck when you don't have anything to numb them with."

The nurse scrunched her nose. "I'm sorry. We have very limited supplies here right now."

Katie pointed at the girl with one of her demons. "Remind me of that later. We need to stock full medical supplies in here."

Stephanie looked at the demons and lifted her eyebrows. "Starting a collection?"

Katie chuckled. "Nope, but I came to get you. You think you can walk?"

Stephanie stood up from the table and headed out of the room. The demons started to struggle again, and Katie stared at them with her angelic eyes. Both of them whimpered slightly, and one softly farted. They went quiet again, pretending that they had fainted.

Katie was fine with that. At least they were silent.

"All the demons have gone back into the portal, and the portal is now shut," the grizzled guard reported to the general.

The general let out a relieved breath so loud the guard

could hear it over the phone. "Excellent. And what was the outcome?"

The guards sounded happy but tired. "We did well. We lost a couple of guards at the beginning, and their bodies are being sent back to the base. All in all, the team won. Katie was really the game changer for us, of course."

"Of course," the general replied.

The guard grunted slightly as he moved his shoulder, which had a long scratch from one of the demons. "The base is pretty roughed up, but the underground facility and the weapons factory are still intact. We are definitely going to need some more men out here, and a cleanup crew would be helpful too. We want to get this place back up to standard fast. They know where we are now, and they know our defenses. We're going to have to change things up."

The general tapped his fingers on the desk, staring at the computer. "Of course, we'll get another group of support personnel out there to you. Whatever keeps the base safe, and the weapons factory safe. The only thing is, we're going to have to move them. We can't support them out in the open like that."

"Absolutely. You just let me know what you need us to do."

The general made a note of it on his clipboard. "Thanks for all your hard work. I'll get back to you soon." He hung up without waiting for a response.

He sat there for a moment thinking, and then picked the phone back up. His secretary came over the line with a sweet voice. "What can I do for you, General?"

The general sat up straight. "Get me the Navy liaison."

16

Stephanie entered one of the medical rooms set up for emergencies. Korbin, Calvin, and Timothy were already there. She walked over next to Korbin and gave him a kiss on the cheek, smiling as best she could. Katie walked in behind her, still dragging the demons by their necks. She kicked the door shut with her foot.

The demons wriggled slightly, but then remembered who Pandora was and went still.

Katie gathered her thoughts, then decided to cut right to the chase. "I know this is weird. I figured I'd give you guys the choice. Stephanie and Korbin? You were Damned before. You fought valiantly today, but it's obvious that we might lose you if you continue this way. So, I brought a couple of knuckleheads to meet you. Knuckleheads, introduce yourselves."

One of the demons raised his scaled head and growled, "Go fuck yourself."

Katie kicked him hard in the back of the thigh, and he collapsed. "Now, that wasn't too nice, was it? I can always let Pandora take me over so she can handle the two of you. I promise you if you aren't put into a body today, you're gonna go back home in a manner so painful you'll be glad to see the fiery depths of hell again."

The demon grumbled and put his head down, rubbing his thigh. "I'm Volruz."

Katie smiled. "Good job. And how about you?"

The demon grumbled and mumbled her name. "Durixath."

"Very good. Well, Vol and Duri, this is Stephanie and Korbin."

Korbin looked at Stephanie and back at Katie. "And these are for us?"

Katie nodded. "If you want them. You're probably the first ever to get a chance to interview your demons and decide if you want to become infected. Anybody have any questions?"

Stephanie studied the female demon from head to foot. "If it's real death or being stuck with me, could you learn to live with it?"

Duri slowly lifted her eyes toward Stephanie. "Depends on how stupid you are."

Timothy put up his hand to stop the proceedings and sashayed forward to inspect the demons. He leaned into Duri. "I don't want my girl Stephanie to be in the same situation I'm in. It's obvious by *those* that you're a girl. And my girl over here? She's in love with that man right there. That's not going to change. So, I want to know—do you like guys?"

Duri smirked and shrugged her shoulders. "I like them in one way when I'm a human and another when I'm a demon. When I'm human, I like to do what all humans do. When I'm a demon, I like to eat them from the bottom up."

Timothy wrinkled his nose and walked back to the group, whispering to Stephanie. Korbin lifted an eyebrow at Volruz. "How about you? Do you like guys?"

Volruz growled loudly and snarled. "Hell, no."

Korbin nodded, pleased with the answer. Calvin put his hand up. "I have a question. What's your preferred food?"

Everyone stared at him strangely and he shrugged his shoulders. "What? My demon's a taco man, which is maybe in the top three foods on the planet. Katie's demon loves donuts. I think it's important. How would you like to get stuck with a demon that only wants tuna, and you hate fish?"

They chuckled, and the tension drained from the room. The two demons grumbled. Katie listened to Pandora confer with them. When she was done, Katie called Korbin and Stephanie over. "Vol is powerful. I mean, he's wicked strong. Duri is incredibly sneaky. They make a really good pair, which is why they worked so well together. I figure if you're gonna have demons and you're in love, you need to have two demons who play well with one other."

Stephanie took Korbin's hand. "That's true. Korbin's the most important person in my life. I don't want anything to come between us."

Katie agreed. "You guys came here at our request and have not asked any questions or for anything from us. Just like you were when you were Damned, you have been self-less. However, if you want to continue to be part of this team, I think you need to make a decision. You could really use the benefits of being Damned. None of us want to see you get injured or worse, and I know that it hit all of us when Stephanie was injured today. To stay with the team, you're going to have to be infected again. It's not the same as becoming uninfected. You won't forget your time together."

Katie could see the relief wash over them. While that made her feel good, some part of her felt terrible for having ripped them back out of the peaceful lives she had put them in. Now they were here, and they knew the group's secrets. Katie felt it was her responsibility to make sure they were as safe as possible. "It's completely up to you. I know you probably need a moment to talk about it, but unfortunately, we don't have long. These two demons won't last forever outside a human body, and I don't think my patience will either."

Stephanie chuckled at Korbin before looking at Katie. "I understand. If you could just give us a few minutes to talk about it, we will let you know."

"Of course. I'll stay here with them and you guys talk. Just let me know what you come up with."

Stephanie and Korbin smiled at Katie as they walked out of the room. As soon as they shut the door behind them, Calvin looked at Katie. "So that was why you jumped through the gates of hell."

Pandora sighed, rolling her eyes. *No, numbnuts, we just wanted a tan.*

"We've got several subs in that area, but subs don't move very fast," the Navy liaison explained.

The general shifted the phone to his other ear. "No, I suppose they don't move quite as fast as a Leviathan. What does that mean for tracking this monster?"

The liaison chuckled. "It means we're doing the best we can. We have to track a monster the size of the Empire State Building underwater. From the outside, that sounds like a simple task, but in reality, it's not. Not to mention the fact that we have to figure out how to kill this thing."

"Yes, have you put any thought into that?"

The liaison sighed. "We could go with conventional missiles, although our fear is that if our ordnance does not penetrate this beast's outer shell, we might just piss it off. We thought about a nuclear option as well. That would involve taking the beast out to deep water and detonating the bomb there. The problem is, we aren't sure how to lure it out there. Not to mention how we keep our soldiers safe after releasing the bomb. We can't just shoot those kinds of bombs from hundreds of miles away underwater. Whoever detonated the bomb would not be coming back."

"Have any attempts been made to take this creature down yet?"

"No, we're just trying to get it back on the radar at this point. Again, we're very hesitant to take action. We want to avoid pissing it off," the liaison explained.

The general thought for a moment and realized he was going to have to bring the mercs into it. "I'll get you specialty torpedoes. However, to make them, I'll need to use a large amount of special metal. I may have to stop making our demon-killing bullets."

"I think the sacrifice will be worth taking this creature

down. You've seen it. He could take New York City down in a half an hour."

"All right. How many torpedoes are you going to need?" The general began taking notes, wanting to make sure he had every bit of information that Katie's team would need.

The liaison thought for a moment. "I would say that we would need at least a dozen. I mean, if that's possible. I want to say that one would work, but we just don't know."

"We could create some sort of special Army packages in them; fashion ball bearings from the special metal that would explode inside the beast's body, poisoning him. That would allow you enough time to use normal torpedoes to rip him apart."

"That's an interesting theory," the liaison replied, although he sounded skeptical.

"We've seen it work in smaller applications with our grenades and bullets. I think that on a large scale it could definitely do the trick," the general assured him.

The liaison filled his lungs with air and held his breath for a moment, deciding. "Let's do it. Make it happen, and let me know what I need to do."

The general made a note on his books and got off the phone with the liaison. He organized his notes quickly and picked the phone back up, calling Katie.

***

Katie sat down on the roof of the building and dangled her feet over the edge. She held a long rope that had been tied around the necks of each of the demons. Pandora had threatened them, and they now seemed resigned to their fate. She was waiting for Korbin and Stephanie to finish their talk and let her know what they wanted to do. She had a feeling that they would want to be on the team, but she had to leave it up to them this time. There would be no more surprises from her. They would make the choices when it came to their life together.

Katie's phone buzzed in her pocket and she pointed a finger at Duri, then Vol. "Not a word." She picked up her phone. "Not. One. Word."

It was the general, and she knew that it had something to do with what had just happened. The last thing she wanted to do was to explain why she was holding two demons. She glowered at them again and pressed the answer button. "General, how are you?"

"Unfortunately, even though I'm celebrating your win, not as well as I would like to be. There's been another attack," the general explained.

"Was it bad? Why didn't you call me?"

The general smirked and waited for her to calm down. "Well, you were kind of in the middle of something. A Leviathan came up from the Mediterranean Sea. He completely devastated a town within fifteen minutes, then disappeared back into the ocean. We've been able to track him on and off. I'm calling because I need a bunch of metal for torpedoes or missiles, or both."

Pandora was listening closely. *Do you mind if I take over? I need to ask him something specific.*

Sure, just let me tell him.

Katie knew that it wasn't the general's favorite thing to talk to Pandora, but she seemed to think it was important.

"Pandora wants to speak with you about this. I think she would be the better person to speak with."

The general nodded. "I agree."

Katie closed her eyes as Pandora took over her body. "General. Leviathans aren't demons as you know them. The metal, even though it is special, probably won't hurt them. So, on the plus side, your regular weapons can be used."

The general groaned. "And what's the downside?"

"Their height. Their scales, which are very tough. I don't know what it will take. They are flame- and heat-resistant too, or at least mostly. It would require a heat hotter than hell's to take them down. Let me ask you this, —which Leviathan is it?" Pandora was slightly fearful of the answer.

The general was annoyed. "How many are there?"

Pandora bit her lip and thought about that. "Seven."

The general closed his eyes and held the phone away, covering the receiver for a moment. "Motherfucking, sonofabitch, bastard demon scum. Fucking with every goddamn thing. If I get ahold of this fucking thing I'm gonna shove that torpedo right up his asshole and press the button my own goddamn self."

He let out a deep breath and panted for a moment, then centered himself and put the phone back to his ear. "I'm back."

Pandora tried to hide a laugh. "Feel better?"

"Yes. Yes, I do. As far as the Leviathan is concerned, from what I saw on the video and what the eyewitnesses have said, he was huge. Taller than any of the buildings he took down, including the resorts. He was scaled, with a long, jagged tail, and apparently he looks like Godzilla. Or she looks like Mrs. Godzilla, or whatever. There was no confirmation on the genitals."

Pandora made a crooked smile with Katie's lips. "That would be a vagina. Her name is Tiamat, and she's a bit of a pain in the puss. I'd suggest bombing the fuck out of her and then salting the ground. Barring that, got any angels around? No? Dude, you are royally fucked."

Katie gave a fake cough. *Did you forget that we are an angel?*

No, we aren't. We are an angel-human-demon hybrid. We are a fucked-up triad at best, but certainly NOT an angel. Besides, you've got quite a ways to go before you start cracking skulls like an angel. I've seen them in action.

The general thought about it for a moment, not realizing that Katie and Pandora were having a conversation. "Can you break her skin?"

Pandora brought her attention back to the general. "Probably. Angel swords will open it readily enough."

Katie got excited. *Ha! Ask him if they have any smaller bombs? Something that packs a big punch in a tiny case?*

Pandora's eye twitched, but she relayed the question. He paused for a moment, slightly confused. "A small bomb? What for?" The general audibly gasped. "You don't want to…*insert* the bomb into this female monster, do you?" He sounded pretty alarmed.

Pandora was silent for a moment, then screamed laughter into the phone. "Teddy Roosevelt on a bicycle, General! Nobody's inserting anything, you sick bastard."

I wouldn't put it past you, Katie mumbled.

Pandora sighed. "Obviously you're aware that Katie has

an angel sword. So, to do this correctly, we would have to fly onto Tiamat's body while others kept her busy. We would cut the bitch with that angelic sword, then shove the bomb into her. I know you're thinking this sounds like a real shit-show. I agree, and I'm not even done yet. After that, we would leave before the bomb explodes. I can promise you, I will be sorely pissed off if we're still on the damn thing when it blows. Riding a tidal wave of flesh and bones is not my idea of a good time anymore."

The general guffawed. "For some reason, I just imagined that—except it was like that picture where the woman is riding a shark with an automatic rifle and a Rambo scarf around her head."

Pandora smirked. "Just be glad that Tiamat isn't *actually* like Godzilla. I'm not sure how to combat laser beams coming out of a giant lizard's mouth. That's not my forte."

The beeping of the sonar from the intel room echoed inside the submarine's cabin as it slowly crept through the water. The crew kept quiet. This was their first encounter with a giant sea monster, and they were all on edge. The captain of the sub walked cautiously back and forth within the tight space. They had been tracking this beast for hundreds of miles and had yet to get a solid signal.

An alarm went off, and one of the sailors jumped up. "Captain, I think we found the dragon, or whatever it is! The sonar shows it swimming very deep about a hundred meters ahead of us."

The captain pointed to one of the other sailors. "Get the general on the line. And Smith, full speed ahead! We're going to chase this thing down. Ready the torpedoes!"

The sailors went to work, scrambling around the small intel room. They were speeding up the sub while trying to aim the torpedoes at what they assumed was the demon.

Whatever it was, it was massive, and it was swimming ahead of them deep beneath the dark water. An alarm sounded again throughout the sub, and one of the sailors scrambled to the intercom. "Battle stations, battle stations! All hands to your posts. This is not a drill! Drop your cocks and grab your socks!"

The captain walked over to the station where FC2 Smith was putting in the coordinates for the torpedoes. "How's it looking?"

The fire controlman looked at the captain and took a deep breath. "We're going to get as close as we can, sir. This thing is moving fast, but we're moving right along with it."

The captain patted him on the shoulder. "Wait for my word."

One of the seamen held up the phone. "I have the general on the line for you."

The captain went over and took the phone. "General Brushwood. We have the beast in our sights, and we have the torpedoes aimed. Do you want us to fire?"

The general thought for a moment. "Until I know our other plan is in place, we're going to continue as instructed. Fire at will."

The captain nodded and handed the phone back to the seaman, going back over to Smith. "Do you have a lock?"

"I do."

The captain looked around for a moment. "Fire."

Smith clicked a switch and pressed the button, and the sub rumbled as it fired twin torpedoes. They watched the sonar carefully as the torpedoes got closer to the beast, finally making contact. The Leviathan let out a roar that could be heard for hundreds of miles. The sonar engineer screamed, ripped off his headphones, and gripped his head. The shockwave rocked the submarine. The crew held on silently as they watched the beast slow.

Smith smiled at the captain. "I think we got it, sir. It's slowing down, and it seems to be sinking lower."

The captain clapped the fire controlman on the back and pumped his fist in the air. "That's how we do it in the Navy!"

Everyone in the room cheered loudly, congratulating each other on a job well done. Smith stayed at his seat, watching the sonar. As the cheers died he stood up, his eyes wide. "Captain?"

The captain turned and immediately the smile fell from his face. It was obvious from the look in Smith's eyes that something had gone wrong. "What is it?"

FC2 Smith shook his head. "I don't think we got it, sir. It has changed course, and it's heading straight for us."

The captain scrambled to the sonar screen. He shouted, "Stop celebrating, you bastards! Fire!"

The submarine fired at the beast, but it only sent the monster off track for a moment. Silt and dirt clouded the water. They reversed engines and began to slow down, just in case there was the chance of an impact. The captain was at a loss for what to do. They had launched their torpedoes, but nothing seemed to break the hard, scaled skin of the Leviathan.

The captain ran over and grabbed the phone. "General, it didn't do any good. It's coming straight at us. We fired all of our torpedoes, and it's still coming—and now it's picking up speed. I'm not sure what else to do. I'm turning the sub at this very moment to avoid running headfirst into it, but we need backup, and we need it now."

The general sent an emergency message over the government's email server. He wasn't ready to get off the phone with the captain, not when they were facing the beast head-on. "I'm sorry, captain, I'll send backup as fast as I can. How close?"

The captain growled at Smith, "How long?"

Smith dropped his hands to his sides and shook with fear. "Three hundred feet and closing sir. It has shifted and is heading for our starboard side. Given the size of it, I don't see how we will make it out of this."

Before the captain could say anything, the general intervened. "Your crew was brave and strong. Thank you for putting your necks on the line for us. We won't forget it."

The captain put his hand over his lips and stared at the young men on his crew. "It was an honor serving with you, general."

The captain hung up and turned to his men. He put a hand on Smith's shoulder and watched the sonar. The gap between the Leviathan and ship closed, and the beast roared.

Smith felt the roar in the pit of his stomach as much as he heard it. Giant claws ripped into the submarine as though it was made of tinfoil, and the crew panicked as water rushed in. The last thing Smith saw was a dark-green hooked claw that pierced his stomach and pinned him to the deck. He held onto the claw and the claw held onto him as the Leviathan pulled the submarine and her crew into the depths of the ocean.

Katie was sitting on the roof contemplating the meaning of life when her captive demons began to growl. She pointed a warning finger at them but looked to see what they saw.

Behind her on the roof, Korbin and Stephanie stood waiting for her. Stephanie smiled. "Everything okay?"

Katie shrugged. "Is anything ever okay in the life of a mercenary? I guess that's not really helpful when you're trying to decide whether to be a Damned, is it?"

Korbin laughed. "It's fine. We know it's not all sunshine and butterflies, and if we didn't know before today, those stitches are definitely proof. Anyway, we're in agreement that we don't want to sit out the fight. We can't just let these demons run the world. We can't watch innocent people die, knowing that we could have done something to help them. We were in this fight for a long time before, and we plan on being in this fight for a long time to come. We want to do it."

The three of them turned to the demons. They were standing there scowling, with the rope around their necks.

Vol scoffed and crossed his boil-covered arms over his chest. "Just because *they* want it doesn't mean *we* do. You can't just tell us to jump into a human. How could you even make us do that?"

Duri obviously agreed. She was glaring at Stephanie with her beady red eyes. "You think that because you're human, you can just decide what happens to us? That's bullshit. You can't make me get inside her. I'm not going to be some human's lackey. I'm not Lilith, and I won't be happy living in a meatsack on Earth."

Katie snarled at them, but she realized that they had a point. She had never thought about the process of putting a demon into someone. Every time a human was Damned, the demon was ready. The human might not have had a choice, but the demon was always ready. Not these two fools. These demons could live on Earth for quite a while, even without nourishment or protection. They weren't like the old demons, who would die within seconds if they weren't inside a body.

Katie reached out to Pandora. *So, maybe there is something wrong with our plan. Do you have any idea how to put these demons into Stephanie and Korbin? I mean, it has to be possible, right? We can keep them inside once they're there.*

Pandora was stumped. *Take them out, sure. But put them in? Nothing.*

Stephanie and Korbin stared at Katie. They knew she was having a conversation with Pandora. Pandora chuckled and readied herself. *Sorry, it's my turn. I forget they can't hear me.*

Pandora took Katie's body over and glared at the demons, who flinched and held onto each other. They didn't want to give in to the humans, but at the same time they didn't want to feel Lilith's wrath. They had heard stories about her when she was in hell—the kind of stories you told your demon children to get them to respect the stronger demons. The only thing they found solace in was the fact that they were on Earth and Pandora was inside a human's body. Kind of.

If it was a choice between dealing with Lilith or infecting Korbin and Stephanie, maybe getting a new meat suit was their best shot.

"I don't want these fucks getting the wrong idea." Pandora tugged on the demon's leash. "Let's get inside and get this show on the road."

When the three mercs and two demons came back inside, Calvin and Timothy had a sudden urge to be elsewhere. They backed out of the room and shut the door behind them. Sure, they were already possessed, but the last thing they wanted was an extra demon. As they left the room, they shooed away all the guards standing outside. Infecting one of them was low on their list as well.

Pandora let go of the leash, since there was no place the demons could go where she couldn't catch them. They stumbled back and struggled to free themselves from the rope, and when they finally did, they snarled at the mercs.

"Cut the shit, fuckwads." Pandora pointed her finger at the two of them. "I know what you're thinking. You're thinking of jumping into the wrong person, aren't you? Let me just set this straight right now. If you try to go into the wrong person, I can promise you that the pain I'm about to cause you will feel like a massage. You will beg me for pain like what you're about to feel if you try to screw with me, or either one of them."

The two demons looked at each other. "What pain?"

Pandora gave Korbin and Stephanie each a kind smile. "You might want to turn around for this. I don't think you actually want to hear it. You would be shocked at how wimpy demons can be when they're being tortured. They're almost worse than humans. I have to give it to humans, they have pretty thick skin—although I don't mean that literally. Humans are basically wrapped in tissue paper. Anything cuts right through them, but they can take a lot of shit and keep their mouth closed. Whoever is torturing them doesn't even get the satisfaction of their screams. It always made me laugh, the way they'd grit their teeth and struggle to stay conscious, but they still wouldn't scream! Half the time I would let the human go just because they were good sports."

Korbin and Stephanie looked at one another, then silently faced the wall. Stephanie plugged her ears with her fingers for good measure.

Calvin, Timothy, and the grizzled guard stood outside the door, discussing repairs to be made to the production building. The battle-hardened guard flinched as a piercing scream rang out from inside of the room. They could hear Pandora cackling wildly. The other demon joined in, howling in pain.

The grizzled guard moved to open the door, but Calvin caught his arm. "Nah, best to wait this one out." Calvin pressed his ear to the door. He heard the soft growl of Pandora's voice. "Yep, Momma still got it!"

Calvin covered his mouth and laughed. The grizzled guard just stared at him with an appalled look on his face. Timothy looked down at his fingernails and yawned, leaning against the wall. "Trust me, she can do a lot more damage than that. She's one hard bitch."

Calvin nodded and glanced at the guard. "He's right. She may be on our side, but she would peel the skin right off of a human if they were fucking with us."

The grizzled guard stood there for a moment without

saying a word, deeply troubled by all this. He began to speak, but couldn't find the words. He sketched a salute to Calvin and walked away.

Several moments of screaming were followed by several moments of silence. The door opened, and Katie motioned for Calvin and Timothy to come into the room. They walked inside to find Korbin and Stephanie curled up on stretchers, completely passed out.

Katie cracked her fingers. "Pandora made them go in, but you know how it is with the whole 'being infected' thing. They pass out when they go in, and they pass out when they come out. Stephanie and Korbin were no different."

Calvin nudged Timothy with his elbow. "Well, we can't leave them sleeping here. We'll put them back in their room so they can get some rest before being welcomed back to the world of the Damned. I'm curious to see what these demons can do with them. They're already two nasty people in a fight."

Timothy struggled to pick up Stephanie. "I thought they both were Damned before. Isn't that where their powers came from?"

Katie moved a piece of hair out of Stephanie's peaceful face. "Sure they were Damned before, but as far as I know neither of their demons did much for them. I don't know a lot about Korbin's demon, but Stephanie's was pretty useless. She helped when Stephanie was injured, but the rest of it was all Mamacita."

Timothy looked down at Stephanie, surprised. "Damn! I'm gonna have to give her some mad props when she wakes up. I thought all that kung fu shit was her demon.

Come to find out, she was my little martial artist with a high-class sense of fashion."

Calvin grunted as he put Korbin over his shoulder. "Korbin's demon was useless. I'm stoked to see what he'll be like after this."

After Timothy and Calvin had disappeared around the corner to Korbin's room, Katie made her way to the elevator. She stretched her arms over her head and then crossed them. She suddenly realized that her armor had disappeared again. She had been so busy dealing with the general and the demons that she hadn't even noticed. At least it wasn't a shock to her system anymore.

The elevator doors opened, and she walked out into the destruction that was her base. The wind had died and the sun had gone behind the horizon, making for a nice warm evening. If it weren't for the toppled buildings and broken cement blocks, it would've been a really beautiful night to walk around the base. It was almost hard to believe that just an hour before there had been hundreds of demons flooding through a giant portal right outside the compound.

Joshua, who was sweeping the area outside of the production building, nodded to her. She smiled and waved back, but rather than talk with him she walked to the landing pad, near the scene of the portal. She stood out in the sand and ash and stared at the sky, wondering where Gabriel actually came from.

"Hey, Gabriel. If you're up there. I could really use a talk with you. Things have gotten a little bit crazy, as you probably know, and I'm not sure which way to turn," Katie pleaded." So, if you can hear me, I'd love it if you would just pop down here for a moment. I'll let you get back to your angel stuff pretty quickly." Katie kept her eyes on the sky as she shuffled along what had been the killing field.

Katie sighed at the stars. She had figured he wouldn't show. He had never told her how to contact him if she needed him, just randomly showed up at the oddest times and handed her halfway useful information. This was the first time she was calling him for help.

Pandora scoffed. *Apparently, angels don't come when you need them. They only come when they want to be creepy or dole out useless information. I can understand why they don't come down every time a human fucks up and asks for help. They would never be able to get their angelic butts back up to wherever they go. You're a big deal, though. Let's be fucking real here. You would think he could take a break from doing whatever he's doing, you know? Put aside washing feet or getting some hot angel-on-angel action or whatever, and come down when you call.*

"You're right, Pandora. She *is* a big deal," a heavenly voice announced from behind them.

Katie spun to see Gabriel standing there. She was absolutely shocked that he had actually come. She had half-expected to go back to her room and then wait two weeks before he made an entrance. Pandora was just pissed, figuring he did it just to show her up or something.

Katie didn't let Pandora come forward. She had a script she wanted to stick to. "Gabriel, thanks for coming. I hope I didn't interrupt you, but something serious is going on. A Leviathan, Tiamat, has surfaced. Not only did it destroy a town, but it's somewhere out in the ocean wreaking havoc on anyone who tries to take it down. Pandora told me I'm pretty much the only one who can deal with it."

Gabriel inclined his head thoughtfully, and put his hands together as if in prayer. His long white hair whipped behind him in the gentle breeze. "I'm aware of the Leviathan. It's a nasty business. I was wondering when they were going to call on you for help. The humans don't really stand a chance against this beast. We were already discussing whether we would have to send out a team of angels. I told them to hold off. I figured you were going to call me eventually."

Pandora grumbled. *You could have just flown down when Tiamat tap-danced all over that city, but I digress.*

Gabriel smirked, letting Katie know that he heard her demon. Katie cleared her throat uncomfortably and shifted her feet. "I don't know that a sword, some armor, and a pair of wings will hurt this thing. It's so big that if I make a wrong move, it just steps on me. I'm toe-jam."

Gabriel stared at her for a moment and then spoke quietly. "What would you ask for?"

Pandora sighed and tilted her head back inside of Katie. *How about some fucking help here? Why does this have to be a hundred questions? He obviously knows what's going on, and yes, I know you can hear me, Gabriel. You know there's a monster attacking and that Katie's the only one who can stop it, yet you're going to make this a teachable moment or some shit! So, she doesn't know what to ask for. Tell her! I swear to God—yeah, that God! It's no wonder demons are taking over Earth. Angels work ass-backward.*

Katie plastered on a huge fake smile and chuckled nervously. *I know you're pissed right now, Pandora, but can you please just let me handle this? Obviously, I would not have asked him here if I didn't seriously need help with this, and right now you are making it worse.*

Pandora huffed. *Fine, fine. Do what you need to do. He wants to know what you need, so go ahead and tell him. A heavenly shotgun? Angelic pepper-spray? You know this is some sort of fucked-up test, so don't complain to me when he answers you with another fucking riddle.*

Katie waved her hand next to her head, trying to clear her thoughts. "Sorry about that. You asked me what I want. Um… A lance, maybe? I don't know. Something that can destroy that creature. I mean, I'd ask for a miracle if I knew what kind of miracles I could ask for."

Pandora mumbled quietly, *How about a miracle to just get rid of the goddamn thing? They sent Lucifer to hell, but they can't get rid of a Leviathan? This is another one of those tests, and I'm failing miserably right now. And part of me wants to scream.*

Gabriel looked at Katie kindly. "Those are interesting things to request, but let me ask you this. Are you trying to get out of this fight?"

Pandora sniffed. *No, she isn't smart enough to ask for that.*

Katie couldn't argue with Pandora. *You might be right on that one.*

Gabriel laughed out loud and put his hands together in front of him nodding. "I can ask."

He cocked his head to the side. Katie just stood there uncomfortably, not really sure what he was doing. He stared at her for several moments with no expression on his face. Finally, he blinked. "You can bring back that which is gone, under the right circumstances."

With that, he disappeared.

Pandora screamed in frustration. *Are you fucking kidding me? After all that? I sat here and said angels talk in riddles, angels don't help when they need to, angels always want to make everything a teachable moment. What does he do? He freaking gives you a riddle. I seriously don't understand what's going on here. I'm telling you right now that if you turn into an angel like Gabriel, I'm going to put you out of your misery. Like, no questions asked. I'll switch to me and snap my own neck.*

Katie tilted her head up to the stars. They twinkled brighter than normal. She let Pandora go off on her rant. She knew from experience there was no stopping her. Gabriel had given her power, she just had no idea what it was. *You can bring back that which is gone under the right circumstances. What does that mean?*

This is literally one of those situations where I'm going to say God only knows, because it's true. Only the crazy winged ones understand that garbage.

Baal lumbered across the office as gently as he possibly could. He was trying not to scare the small demon too badly. He wanted information from the little guy, but the kid was so terrified that he could barely put two words together without bursting into tears. He had to admit, it was the first time he had seen a demon crying in a very long time.

"You were there when Katie entered hell, weren't you?" Baal asked.

The small demon shook his head nervously, nearly vibrating in the chair. "No, sir. I mean yes, sir. I saw her come in, but I was on the other side of the gate so I couldn't get to her."

Baal waved his hands, trying to calm the boy. "No, no. I'm not here to punish you for not killing her. I'm trying to figure out exactly what happened. Most of the demons who were anywhere close to her were dead when I got back. I can't really ask them anything, can I?"

The young demon shook his head and shifted in his chair. "I suppose not."

Moloch creaked the door open and stepped inside, moving to the other side of the room behind the desk. He was curious to see what the demon knew, or at least could remember from that time. Baal ignored Moloch and walked in circles around the demon with his claws flashing.

"And what do you remember her doing once she was inside the gate?"

The demon glanced at Moloch and then back at Baal. "I don't really know. I mean, I saw so many things, but it was complete chaos inside the gate. There were hundreds and hundreds of demons fleeing back to hell, and then there were the ones attacking her. I think I saw two get knocked out, but I don't remember exactly who they were. To be honest, I was just trying to get back to hell myself. I've been trapped outside of the gate before, and it hurts like a motherfucker to be shot by those bullets." The little guy's nose was running. He wiped a glob of snot from his upper lip.

Baal walked behind the young demon and put his claws on the demon's skinny shoulders. "Sure, I understand. I don't blame you at all for being afraid. Those humans can be pretty tough. What I need you to do for me now is, I need you to be brave. I need to enter into your mind to understand the nuances of what happened and see how hell affected the human. This is vital information."

The demon was tense. Though he didn't really want the demon in his head, he couldn't tell him no. "Will it be painful?"

"No," Baal lied. He patted the small demon on the head.

The demon exhaled and visibly relaxed into the chair.

"Not painful. Not…" Baal ran his hands up to the demon's head and twisted it right off his shoulders. He left the body in the seat and cracked the head on his knee. He opened the skull like a coconut and began eating the demon's brains. He wiped gooey black blood from his chin and tossed the pieces of skull back into the demon's lap. He patted the demon on his dead shoulder. "Not very."

Moloch chuckled and leaned back in his chair, waiting for Baal to let him know what he had learned. Baal finished swallowing the rest of the brains and plopped down in the seat across from Moloch. He licked blood off his fingertips. "From the memories I see, it doesn't seem like anything really happened to her. She knocked the demons out and dragged them back out of hell, for whatever reason. The only thing I can't figure out is that it doesn't actually seem like Pandora was the one messing with the gate."

Moloch raised a claw to his peeling lips and stared into space. "If it wasn't her, then who was it?"

Katie went back inside the bunker, Gabriel's words floating through her head. Pandora was on a roll now. She had a thousand different interpretations of what Gabriel's comment could've really meant.

Maybe he meant, like, you can bring back the old mercenary team. You know, since Korbin and Stephanie are here. Or maybe he meant that you could bring back the guys you killed with your vagina.

Katie rolled her eyes. *That was one guy, but thanks for bringing it up.*

Ooh, maybe you can bring back your virginity. That's probably been gone quite a while.

Under what circumstances would I want that back? Katie couldn't help but smirk as she rode the elevator down.

Maybe you are meant to birth the next Jesus or something.

Pandora, I think this has more to do with memories than a virgin birth or anything about my vagina.

Pandora cackled. *Maybe it means bringing back the sex drive I stole from our black Superman, Calvin. It's possible he was just looking out for his guys.*

Katie ignored her and walked down the hall. She stopped outside of Stephanie and Korbin's room. The door was open, and Stephanie was standing in front of the mirror peeling the gauze from her side. She looked at Katie and tried to smile.

"I just woke up, and it's crazy. The slashes are already beginning to heal." Stephanie marveled at the cuts. She could almost see them mending.

Katie nodded and came in. "That tends to happen when you have a demon inside you. They don't like to be in pain, and they usually work to heal your body faster because you're pretty much their lifeline."

As Katie talked to Stephanie, Pandora tapped into the demon. *How you doing in there, Duri?*

She grumbled. *It's cramped.*

Yeah, you'll get used to that. I just wanted to stop by and give you the lowdown on what's going on. You have a human now, and you're not to control this one. You need to work really hard to protect her. If you do that for her, she'll do it for you. I've worked with her before, and she's a bad mamma-jamma.

Mamma what? Duri sighed. *What will I get out of it?*

The question is not what you would get out of it, but rather what will happen to you if you don't. On pain of the final death, remember that. T'Chezz was never seen again. You want to be the second demon killed forever in this century? Your best buddy can be number three.

Duri didn't answer, but from the fear Pandora felt surging from her she didn't have to. Katie helped Stephanie put the gauze back around her wounds and sat down beside her on the bed. Korbin must have already woken up, because he wasn't in the room. Katie smiled at Stephanie and took her hands. "Do you want to participate in a test?"

Stephanie grinned at her. "What kind?"

Katie shrugged. "I've no idea. It's just a hunch."

Stephanie stared at her curiously for a moment and then nodded, knowing she could trust Katie. Katie situated herself, then lifted her hands and placed them on Stephanie's forehead. Her red eyes faded into bright blue points. Stephanie fell into those eyes.

Katie reached out with her mind, trying to get her abilities to flow into Stephanie. It was incredibly important to her that she help Stephanie get her memory back. When she had first separated Stephanie and Korbin from the Damned life, she thought those memories would be nothing but painful. Now that the two of them had rejoined the team, Katie realized that the memories were part of Stephanie and Korbin. The memories were who they were. Those memories would help them in the future, especially now that they were Damned again and ready to walk into battle.

After several moments Stephanie blinked and glanced at Katie. Katie pulled her hand away and looked deep into her eyes. "Did it work? Do you have any memory of the past?"

Stephanie gave her a kind smile. "I wish I could say yes, but I don't remember anything that I didn't remember before."

Katie plopped her hands back in her lap, frustrated that

it hadn't worked. She bit her lip and looked around the room, trying to reason out exactly what it was that she was supposed to do. She knew that the message from Gabriel was about giving Stephanie and Korbin their memories back, but beyond that, she had no idea what she was doing.

Stephanie put her hand on Katie's cheek. "It's okay. Maybe those memories are supposed to be gone. We'll just have to get used to being Damned. If we did it once, we can do it again."

Katie stood up from the bed and paced the floor. "No, you are supposed to have these memories. I was given a gift, I think. I'm supposed to be able to give you your memories back. I just don't know how to do it."

Katie walked over to the dresser and put her palms down on it, then closed her eyes and concentrated. Fluttering through her mind were visions of things that had happened in the past. They were events that Stephanie and Korbin had both been involved in. Katie began to whisper those events out loud. She thought of one. She walked over next to Stephanie. "Close your eyes."

Stephanie did.

Katie sat down and regarded Stephanie with a smile. "There was one fight I remember. We had gone looking for it. You and I, we ended up in a bar, and took out pretty much every demon in the place until we found the one we were looking for. Korbin didn't like that we were going out like that, but it was what we were made to do."

Stephanie looked at her strangely. She felt a tingle in her chest that began to pour throughout her body, heating her body like sparks against kindling. "Keep talking."

Katie crossed her legs and put her hands on her knees.

She concentrated on the spinning fan overhead. "You were so brave. You were always brave, even the first time I met you. Then we put that succubus in you, and you were unstoppable. I think you and Korbin had already fallen in love by that point, but you didn't want to admit it to each other."

As Stephanie listened, visions formed. Neurons started to reconnect in her mind. There were flashes of things she hadn't remembered before. They were like tiny movie reels all going off at the same time until they eventually slammed together into one large memory.

Stephanie gasped for air and grabbed Katie's knee, then opened her eyes and looked at Katie with a smile. "I remember! I remember every beat of my heart during that time. I remember every heartbreak and excitement, and I remember all of you."

Tears streamed down Stephanie's face as she giggled, the private memories between her and Korbin flooding back to her. It was like finding herself all over again, and this time everything made so much more sense. Katie leaned over and hugged her tightly. She set her chin on Stephanie's shoulder. "I'm sorry those memories were lost until now."

Stephanie leaned her head against Katie's. "Don't be sorry. I understand why, now."

A gentle knock came on the door, after it creaked open, Timothy flounced into the room. He stopped in his tracks and looked at Stephanie and Katie, face full of concern. Stephanie laughed and jumped up, then threw her arms around Timothy. "I need one of those girls days out so badly right now."

Timothy leaned back and looked her in the face, confused at first, but then excited. "My baby is back!"

Katie smiled and stood up. "I'll go get Korbin set up."

She brushed past Calvin, who was standing in the doorway. He had been behind Timothy the whole time, and could see that the memories were back. "If you give me a minute, I'll come with you. I want to see you give the old man his game back."

Pandora sniffed. *Well, that was fucking heartwarming. Now the old man and his broad can remember everything. I guess it's better than having to explain something to them every five seconds.*

Katie grinned. *You really know how to make a moment special, don't you?*

Hey, remember that I'm a demon. We don't come with a mushy side.

Katie was about to disagree with her when her phone rang. She looked down at it and saw the general's number on the screen. "General Brushwood, what's going on?"

The general cleared his throat. "You know how I told you that the Navy was tracking the Leviathan?"

Katie nodded her head. "I do. How's that going?"

After a deep sigh and a few moments of contemplation, the general finally told her. "There was a submarine in the Mediterranean. They found the beast, but the beast found them, too. Pandora was right—firing conventional torpedoes at that thing is like throwing stones at a steel box. They didn't do a damn thing. In the end, the sub was lost with all hands. It was tragic and we're mourning the loss of those sailors."

"Jesus, did they even do her any harm?" Katie asked.

The general didn't want to say it because he knew Pandora had already told him. "A little, but not enough to keep her from turning on them. Do you have any ideas? Well, I guess does Pandora have any ideas on how to take her down?"

Pandora took over Katie's voice. She was getting better at switching back and forth with her. "First you find it, then you make it go where you have any kind of chance of surviving. It's preferable that you go somewhere that you can assure the least amount of casualties. Then you kill it."

"But how do you find it? The Navy, and not just the US but all the navies of all the major powers, are working this angle." The general groaned with exhaustion.

Pandora was trying to remember what she knew about the Leviathan from her time in hell. "But, the issue is in the sea. It has an advantage we know about there. Tiamat is intelligent, and knows the demon language." She brightened. "Hey, what about smack talking her?"

The general went quiet, then scoffed. "You want to piss off a giant dragon monster by talking smack to her? I'll have to get back to you on that."

Katie took back over before Pandora could get smart with the general. "I know it sounds crazy, General, but think about what Pandora said. We're not saying you should talk smack to the Leviathan for no reason, but if it's intelligent, maybe it's hunting something. Maybe it's hunting us, me or Pandora. Taunting it might be our only way to get it out of the ocean so that we have a chance of fighting it."

The general still wasn't sold. "I'll work on it. It just seems like a crazy idea, you have to understand that."

Katie sat quietly for a moment but knew there was no time to waste, even in the wake of disaster. "General, make the plans and we'll be there. We *will* take her down. I promise."

Katie and the general hung up. She closed her eyes and shook her head. *I'm not sure he thinks that is the best way to handle this problem.*

Pandora forced a chuckle. *It's Tiamat. There* is *no best way to handle that bitch.*

Down deep in the bowels of hell, Moloch and Baal didn't seem to have a care in the world. They sat in Moloch's office with their feet propped up on the table, munching on the day's catch of baby bunnies. Moloch reached out and grabbed a bunny by the ears, holding it over his mouth and dropping it inside with a crunch. Baal ate them a little bit more neatly, holding one by his fluffy tail and taking off the head first.

Moloch grabbed the remote, clicking on the television to watch the human news report. "I'm so glad they got American cable down here. It makes keeping up with the humans a lot easier."

Baal nodded with a full mouth. "I also like that show, what's it called? With the dad, his weird friend, and his four daughters."

Moloch laughed. "Oh yes, *Full House*. I hear there's a new one out."

"No shit," Baal exclaimed, chunks of bunny and fur flying from his open mouth.

"Oh, oh, shh! The news is on, and it looks like our baby has made headlines," Moloch bragged. He sat up and put his terrible chin in his twisted hands, captivated.

On the screen, a newscaster was playing several different YouTube videos from the attack on the Mediterranean beach town. The two demons laughed wildly as they watched the Leviathan destroying the town through a shaky lens. The news had blacked out some of the carnage, which pissed Moloch off, but he was just happy to see that the Leviathan had done her job.

The reporter came back onto the screen, her face white. "This is a special report by News Seven. The same creature that can be seen in these YouTube videos, the instigator of the Mediterranean beach carnage, has struck again. Reports are flooding in that the monster has destroyed an American submarine. From what the military is saying, all hands were lost."

Moloch and Baal looked at each other and fist bumped, having gotten exactly what they wanted out of the Leviathan. "Well, it seems that Tiamat was worth all that trouble it took to get her there."

Baal nodded and fist-bumped him again. "You know, I think the fist bump is probably the best method the humans ever created of displaying happiness. Fuck all that hugging and crying and shit. Everybody should be fist bumping."

Moloch took a deep breath and stood up from his chair,

nodding at Baal. "I agree. Now, I think we should talk about Katie and her recent antics here in hell. Any thoughts on why she would have demon-napped those two idiots? I mean, there are plenty of demons on Earth. Why come all the way to hell to do it?"

Baal shrugged his shoulders. "I haven't figured it out yet. And nobody else seems to know anything about those two, besides the fact that they worked well together, and they were kind of trouble. I've tried talking to Lucifer, but he's been busy."

Moloch rapped his fists on the windowsill as he gazed out over the lava pits of hell. "I don't like this. I don't know what she's up to, but with Pandora being such a conniving backstabbing bitch, I can only imagine it's going to be something big."

Baal rolled his eyes and put a lid on the bunnies. "Not to mention that it's probably going to bite us in the dick before we figure it out."

Moloch shook his finger at the demon. "We need to go talk to Tiamat. She's our best chance on Earth right now. We failed to get the weapons, so we're just going to have to go another route. With Katie and Pandora out there, I'm thinking it's going to be very difficult to get our hands on that ammunition or the ammunition maker, for that matter. We need to see if the Leviathan will go to New York for us."

Baal laughed loudly. "They probably won't even notice her with all the monsters running around that shithole."

20

The guards and the mercenaries worked diligently on the base, trying to get it back in order and ready themselves for whatever would come next. Between having Katie back on base and having Korbin and Stephanie there, everyone was in a good mood. They had no doubt in their minds that they could handle whatever hell threw at them.

"These bastards aren't going to get away with this a second time. They already destroyed one of my bases, and now they've come for this one. I'd like to see them come back now that I have my memories. I have something to give them," Korbin snarled.

Calvin looked at him, curious. "What's that?"

Korbin put up his fist. "My fist up their fucking asses."

Calvin laughed. "Calm down, old man. I don't think you actually want to put your fist up their asses. You don't know where those demons have been."

Everyone chuckled, but Korbin kept a straight face just like he always had in the past. Now that he could remember all the heartbreak and struggle he had been through, he was even more pissed. Everyone there believed they had the situation under control. That they could face anything that came their way and take it down, just like they had on the base the day before.

Katie walked into the room and pulled the phone to the center of the table. "I've got the general on the line, and I'm going to put him on speaker."

Everyone gathered around the table and Katie pressed the intercom button. "Go ahead, General. We are all here."

The general was in the same kind of mood—ready to do some work, kill a few demons, and get everyone to safety. "Korbin, Stephanie it's good to hear that you're back. Now, I've got some orders. You're going to have a metric fuck-ton of boots on the ground as we wrap up your base and move you. We need to get everything secure and safe. I don't want you guys to worry about that. Focus your attention on important things. The demons know where you are, and they know where your weaponry is. The secret's out, and unfortunately, that means you can't stay, at least not right now."

Korbin pounded his fist into his hand. "This is bullshit. How do they keep finding us? There had to be somebody on the inside. As far as I know, no one but you and our team knew where we were located and that the weapons were here."

The general sighed. "Unfortunately, I'm sure there is a leak. But there has been a leak for a long time if you think about it. Nothing goes easy here, especially when you're dealing with politicians and demons—some of which are wrapped up in one annoying package. We can worry about that later, though. For now, my men are on their way. They're ready to get going."

Katie cut in. "General, what can we do to help? Should I stay out here with the team and escort them to wherever they're going?"

The general chuckled. "Unless you would like to help the movers, I suggest leaving."

Katie smirked. "I think I've done enough moving in my day. I'll let you guys handle it."

Calvin offered, "I'm gonna stay here with Korbin to get him up to speed. There's a lot of things he's missed since he's been gone, and I want him to be on the right page. Before everything gets packed up, I think we should start going through it. On top of that, I want to be here and watch as they are moving these things. I want to make sure that we can trust everyone. After that, I'll meet you in New York."

"I've made sure that all these boots have been vetted, but Calvin, you're right. Someone should be there just to keep an eye on things. Obviously, we can't trust everyone," the general admitted.

Katie took a deep breath and looked around her. She didn't believe that they were going to have to move yet again. She was glad that she had already taken up residence in New York and had a place for everyone. Otherwise, she might just go crazy trying to get everyone situated all over again. "All right, general, you know how to get hold of me. I'm going to make some arrangements and then head to New York. Thank you for sending the troops."

"Absolutely, Katie. You guys are our hope for the future, but you don't have to do it alone." The general was honest and kind. Everyone could tell that he had changed over the years.

Katie hung up the phone and looked at the others. She was sad that she was going to be away from them for a little while. She had gotten used to having her family back, but things needed to get done. There was a Leviathan trying to kill everyone. "Timothy, if you could call the plane to pick me up I would appreciate it."

Timothy nodded and collected his things. Calvin chuckled, then eyed her suspiciously. "You mean you're not going to fly back to New York with those wings?"

Katie rolled her eyes and slapped Calvin on the back of the head. "Don't be jealous. I know it was no surprise that I had an angel in me. This is just one of the perks."

Calvin leaned back and laughed loudly. "I think it's less of a shock that you have a demon in you. I feel like the angels made a mistake. Who gives majestic wings and sweet shining armor to a demon like Pandora?"

Pandora growled. *Watch it. I can still control your dick.*

<hr>

"*Sí, mamá, te lo haré saber. Sí, estoy comiendo. De acuerdo, hablaré contigo más tarde. Te quiero. Adiós.*" The young college kid hung up the phone and looked at his roommate, embarrassed.

"Aw, Chrissy, your mama misses you?" his roommate teased.

"I'm still in Spain, but she acts like I've moved to the moon. It's college! She had eighteen years to prepare for this." Chris shook his head and laughed.

Both the guys plopped down on a futon in the small common area of their dorm. Manuel grabbed the remote and clicked on the television, not paying attention to what was on the screen. "Chris, you gotta cut your mom some slack. You're her baby. Trust me, after a while she'll be glad to have some quiet in the house."

Chris opened a bag of chips and popped a Dorito in his mouth. "I guess. Or she'll just haunt me for the rest of my life."

Manuel laughed and nodded at the television. "What's this?"

Chris shrugged his shoulders. "Looks like they made some kind of new Godzilla movie. I didn't hear anything about this at theaters. It looks like there's a lot of money in it."

Manuel leaned forward, entranced by what was going on. "I didn't hear anything about it either. Damn! Look at those special effects."

Chris tipped the bag of Doritos into his mouth and spoke, spraying crumbs. "I know, right? The actors are so real. And it looks like it was filmed right on the coast of Spain. Crazy that I didn't hear anything about it."

"Dude, watch the extras in the background. You would think they all went to Juilliard or something. That must've cost the producers a fortune."

Chris knocked cheese dust from his hands. "Man, can you imagine? Getting cast as an extra in a movie where you could make rent just by running from nothing. They put the CGI dude in later. Seriously, I need to start going out on casting calls or something. I need some extra cash."

Manuel looked at him sideways. "Please, your mother

sends you money all the time. Besides, you're not an actor. Aren't you going to school for animation?"

Chris nodded his head. "Yeah, but I'll do anything to get my foot in the door. Though I'm pretty sure it took a thousand people a million hours to animate that giant monster. It's so lifelike. You can see all the muscles moving in its legs as it stomps around. They even made sure to put the blood on the ground wherever it smashes somebody with its tail. That's some crazy shit. One day, my name will be on the credits for a movie like this. Some real James Cameron shit."

They sat there watching as Tiamat attacked the coast of Spain, ripping through the boats at the shore and demolishing building after building. It was the same result as the Mediterranean beach town, only this was larger with a lot more carnage. Every time a building collapsed or a body was ripped in half the guys would grimace, but then high five each other. They still could not believe how lifelike it looked.

Manuel picked up the remote and clicked on the guide, trying to find the name of the movie. "It's not listed here. The guide says it's the news, and this doesn't even have anything listed in the spot. I think it's crazy they have something this bloody on one of the regular channels anyway."

Chris grabbed a bag of Cheetos and went to town. "It's a new era, baby. They are letting all kinds of stuff on regular channels now. Before you know it, we'll flip on channel five at three o'clock in the afternoon and there will be porn."

Manuel chuckled and tossed the television remote at

Chris. "Man, you wish. Like you don't get enough porn. I'm always nervous to walk in here. I have to prepare myself to see all kinds of crazy shit you pull up off the Internet."

Chris's face went serious. "Hey, I'm just studying the human form."

Manuel barked a laugh. "If you are so worried about studying the human form, maybe you should stop watching porn and go out on a date."

"Oh, shit! That monster just crashed through the building and grabbed those poor fucks right out of their seats. That's like a million hours of rendering just right there." Chris pointed at the television, marveling at the magic of modern technology.

Just then there was a knock on the door and Manuel rose. He kept his eyes glued to the television as he walked over and answered it. One of his friends rushed in, sweating and out of breath. "Are you guys watching the attack on Spain? It's fucking crazy, right? First demons, and now monsters coming out of the ocean and just demolishing shit!"

Manuel and Chris eyed each other for a moment and glanced back at the television as the monster grabbed three people off the ground. Blood sprayed as the monster ripped their heads off. On screen, the monster's claws were stained red.

Chris swallowed hard and put the bag of Cheetos back down. He stared at the cheese dust coating his hands, staining them orange.

"Anyway, I just want to let you guys know that classes are canceled for the rest of the afternoon because of this," the kid mumbled, and backed out the door.

Manual and Chris sat there in silence for several moments.

Manuel began, "The guide said it was the news."

"Yeah, it did."

"The guide didn't say movie."

"No, it didn't."

Manuel cleared his throat and clicked off the television. He turned to Chris. "I think we can agree that we're just never going to speak of this again…ever."

21

K atie didn't mind the plane ride so much. It gave her some time to think and sort through things. She had been going nonstop for as long as she could remember, and after the recent battles, her mind was exhausted. Pandora seemed to be doing the same thing, keeping quiet throughout the whole flight except when she complained about being hungry.

Katie looked out the window as they landed at the airport and Pandora let out a deep sigh. *Finally, we're back in the city. I never thought I'd say that after living on the base for so long, but I could use some luxury, and our condo has that.*

I couldn't agree more.

Katie gathered her things and exited the plane. She had them store everything she had brought back with her. She wasn't in the mood to lug a whole bunch of ammo and weapons back to her condo. Initially, she was going to grab a cab back to the condo, but traffic was a bitch, so she made her way to the edge of the airport pick-up area and took off from there, using her wings to get her home.

She landed about a block away in an alley so as to not make a big stink with her angel wings. She rolled her shoulders and folded them back, and they disappeared before she walked out of the alley.

Pandora groaned. *Looks like we no longer just have fans of your work. From the strange new people I see gathered outside, some people want to see you back in the gateway to hell.*

Katie frowned at the people walking back and forth in front of the condo. They had gotten creative and now carried elaborate signs. Some of them were positive, calling Katie an angel and the savior of the city, while others were decidedly more negative.

Katie chuckled. *Don't Trust the Demon, She'll Take Us Down. That's a creative sign. And all this time I thought I was helping people.*

Humans are weird. Even when you're saving their lives, if you don't conform to what they think you should be, the fuckers turn on you. I've seen it time and again throughout history.

They will change their tune the next time I save somebody's life, and it happens to be theirs. Oh, well, I guess I'll go around back.

Katie snuck around the corner of the block and made her way to the back of the building. She used the guard's key to open the service door and ride the elevator back up to her suite. When she walked in, Angie was sitting cross-legged on the couch making notes on a legal pad.

Angie looked up with a smile. "Welcome home. I was actually just working on a couple of things for us."

Katie dropped her bag and collapsed into a chair. "Oh, yeah? Like what?"

Angie put down the pad of paper. "I scoped out a couple

of places that could be test sites for the project. There's a place in Brooklyn, and another place uptown."

Katie managed to grab a handful of candy from the jar on the table without moving from the chair. "How's everything going? Is it still effective?"

"Oh yeah, very effective. Though I have to say, with the exception of the incursion on your base, it's been kind of quiet. We were starting to think it wasn't working, but we realized there has just been a serious decline in gate openings around New York right now. We're not worried though. It's sure to pick up. Regardless of how few and far between they become, this system is important."

Katie listened intently. "Do you think we still need test sites?"

Angie tilted her head back and forth thinking about it. "Honestly? I do. Even if they don't make the system any better, it'll help people on the ground. That's what's most important."

"Same deal as New York City, but for less time."

Angie bit her bottom lip, thinking about something else. "Is my boss going to take down Godzilla?"

"Tiamat," Katie replied.

"Beg pardon?"

Katie grabbed the whole jar of candy this time. "The monster's name is Tiamat, according to Pandora. And she's a real bitch."

Pandora snickered. *Maybe she's like the commercial. Just feed her a bunch of donuts or a bunch of Snickers and she'll turn back into a blue whale or some shit.*

"So, the beast is no longer on your sonar?" the general asked.

The captain on the other end of the line swallowed nervously. "No, she slipped back into deep water. We've picked up signals from her here and there. We have a general understanding of where she is. She's also bleeding from some of the hits by the jets, so that helps us."

The general tapped his pen on his desk. The screen in front of him showed the most recent YouTube video of the attack on Spain. "Good. I want you to make sure that you follow her as far as you possibly can."

"Can she regenerate?" the captain asked.

The general rubbed his hand over his face. "I honestly don't know, but I can contact my source. I'll find out if they have any information on the healing times for this beast."

The chief of staff broke in over the other two men. "We need to make sure that if it has a quick healing time, we continue to beat at it while it's injured. Maybe we can keep it down long enough that it doesn't launch another attack. That should give us time to formulate a full-scale plan."

Several other of the people on the line mumbled back and forth to each other, but the general couldn't make out what they were saying—nor did he really care. There was so much going on and so much he didn't understand that frustration had set in. So had exhaustion. He thought he finally had a handle on the demons and how to tackle them, no matter what they threw at him. Then this thing showed up and took him right back to the square one.

The general spoke loudly over all the other voices. "If that's all, I need to get on the phone with my source. You know how to contact me."

The general might have hung up, but the others were still there. There was silence for several moments, and then someone asked, "What rock did he find a source under?"

Someone else chuckled. "Probably some crotchety old professor of ancient history or something."

The general sat at his desk for several moments rubbing his hands over his face. He was frustrated by everything at that point, but he needed to keep on going. He picked up the phone and gave Katie a call.

Katie answered quickly. "What's up?"

The general groaned. "More issues with the Leviathan. I actually have a few questions. Now they're not just coming from me, but from some of the higher-ups."

Katie wasn't sure what the general wanted, but she knew she wasn't going to be much help. "You should probably talk to Pandora on this one. I know how much you love that."

The general grumbled, "I have to do what I have to do. People's lives are at stake here, and every second that passes that Leviathan is growing stronger. We were able to get in a few good hits when it attacked Spain, but I don't know how long that will keep it down. So yes, I need to talk to Pandora. Please."

Katie was in the middle of eating a huge sub and replied through a mouthful of six different types of meat and cheese. "Sure, hold on one second."

The general sat there for a moment listening to her chew, and when she was done, Pandora's voice came over the phone. "How's it hangin', big shot?"

The general chuckled. "I have some questions about the Leviathan."

Pandora took a bite of the sandwich, chewed, and swallowed. "Shoot."

"I need to know whether Tiamat can regenerate." He was not really sure he wanted to know the answer.

"Yes, but not as fast as I can heal Katie. She just needs a lot of food to regenerate." Pandora tore into the sandwich. "Hungry bitch, so look out for snack time. She isn't demonic."

"And there are seven of them?"

Pandora smirked. "As far as you know, yes."

The general's voice grew high and strained. He was slightly frustrated. "Well, are there?"

Pandora put down the sandwich. "What's the consulting rate for this call?"

The general sighed. "How much?"

Pandora knew how to play the game, even if she couldn't get Katie to do it on a regular basis. "How about a favor? Someday I may ask for something. That day may never come, but let's be honest, I'm going to ask eventually. Nothing too onerous for a human. No butt stuff. Deal?"

The general thought about it for a second, and realized he really didn't have any other options. "With reservations, I agree."

When Katie was done eating her giant sub, she threw away the trash and headed back to her room. She had every intention of just relaxing on her bed. She felt the tension growing inside of her. She couldn't tell whether it was coming from everything going on or from Pandora, but it made her antsy.

Why can't I ever just relax?

Pandora snickered. *Probably because I can't relax, and we're very in tune with each other. Maybe if you got laid you could relax? I don't know, I'm not a doctor. But maybe if you got a nice hard—*

Nope. Katie leaned back on the bed and rolled her eyes. *Not this again. With everything going on right now, the last thing I need is something romantic.*

Who said shit about romance?

Even if that romance only lasts one night. What I need is quiet. A few minutes of peace. Hell, I don't know what I need. I just know that no matter what I do, I can't seem to relax.

Maybe it's the angel inside you. They don't sleep, kind of like us. The difference is, they want you to save Earth, and I just want to kick some demon's dick into the dirt.

Katie shook her head. *I'm pretty sure you want to save Earth too. You just don't want to admit it. You wouldn't be so enthralled with those superhero movies if you didn't.*

Pandora gasped excitedly. *I have an idea. Since you can't seem to relax anyway, you might as well get rid of some of that energy.*

Pandora, I'm not going to go out and find a man. Give up.

Pandora hissed, *That's not what I'm talking about. What I am talking about is playing a little vigilante hero.*

A hero. Katie sat up in the bed and shrugged. *Hell, why*

not? It's not like you're going to let me relax. I might as well fly around and kick some villain's teeth out. Maybe that'll get some of the energy out of my system. Let me just suit up.

Katie hopped out of bed and pulled out her normal hunting outfit, pulling the stretchy Lycra material over her body and strapping the holsters around her waist. She picked up two of her guns and slammed them home. *No donuts?*

Pandora blew a raspberry. *Maybe after. Right now, I'm ready to take some motherfuckers down.*

Pandora had complete control of Katie's body, and she grinned as she soared from rooftop to rooftop. They hadn't done any vigilante work, but Katie was trying to let Pandora have her fun. Besides, all the flying was definitely using up some of her energy. Katie would crash hard when they got back home, which was a good thing. She hadn't slept well in weeks.

Pandora landed on the edge of a building and looked down at the street. *Na na, na na, na na, na na, na na, na na, na na, na na... Slut Girl! Slut Girl!*

Katie scoffed inside Pandora's head. *Oh, hell no. Are you fucking kidding me? Of all the hero names you could have come up with, you had to come up with Slut Girl? Did you actually think that I would go for that? I will not allow you to call me that.*

Pandora grumped. *I guess I'll just be Katie Fucking Lame Twat, then. What a fucking letdown.*

Hey, I'm pretty sure other people don't think that being called

Katie is a letdown. I think you should probably be happy with just regular Katie.

Pandora sat down on the edge of the building and kicked her feet like a super-powered two-year-old who didn't get her way. *I need a secret identity. You already run around in sexy tights wearing guns. You take all the excitement out of it. You've left nothing for me.*

Katie tried to hold back a chuckle. *You do realize that you're the one who created my whole persona, right? You're the one who insisted on tight spandex, and you're the one who turned me into a lean, mean, demon-slaughtering machine. Before that, it was volleyball uniforms, tight ponytails, and fried foods that did not leave my hips.*

Pandora snickered. *Oh, I remember. I have nightmares about it all the time. I guess if you're not going to go along with whatever I want to call you, then I'm going to have to come up with a secret identity of my own. Maybe something like...MiMi? I could run around in a granny outfit. Slippers and robes? But that would suck because then I would look all gross and nobody would pay attention to a gross old lady flying through the air.*

They would pay attention, but it would be for comic purposes and to put on YouTube. No one would believe it was real. And if you used my wings, I'm pretty sure they would figure out that it was me. How many old ladies, or young ladies, for that matter, do you see running around the city with angel wings?

Pandora put her hand on her chin and looked out over the city. *Good point. I can just go as Vampirella?*

Katie groaned, regretting letting Pandora ever see those damn comic books. The ones she loved were drawn by men. The skimpier the outfit, the more heroic she thought the hero was.

Katie didn't feel like arguing anymore, but she knew that if she didn't clear this up, she would end up in a really bad situation. *Okay, I appreciate the fact that you are being creative as hell here, but I'm not wearing a G-string bathing suit as a superhero outfit.*

But lady, you are the only human alive with the tits to do it! Seriously, the rest of the humans I've seen are malformed goblins. Their boobs are either way outlandish, those big plastic jiggly ones that make them topple over but probably double as life preservers, or they have teeny tiny titties. Let's face it, nobody wants to see a superhero running around in a bathing suit with a flat chest.

Here's an idea. How about you stop making it about the body and make it about how productive we can be as a vigilante? People will pay attention to us even if we're fully clothed as long as we actually start solving crimes. We get nothing if we keep sitting on top of buildings talking about our outfit. Katie could sense danger close by, but she was letting Pandora take the lead.

Pandora pouted. *We still need to discuss the outfits later. You never had much fashion sense, anyway. I'm the one who had to fold that into you. I suppose I could try to be somewhat family-friendly. I don't think it would go over as well if I dropped in to save some kids and a tit fell out of my shirt.*

Katie laughed. *No, I don't suppose it would. And I can already see it. Your heroic stance. The flop of the boob. The flash of a camera. We would be having a Janet Jackson moment in the middle of New York City.*

Pfft, you know Janet didn't mind that. She got some serious press out of it, too. Be proud of those melons, Janet.

Katie shook her head, then stared down into the alley,

trying to focus Pandora's attention there. *So, can we actually do some vigilante work? Or we can just go back home so I can go to sleep?*

Pandora leaned over the edge and saw three men in the alley. Two younger, tattooed men had guns drawn, and they were pointing them at a kindly-looking older gentleman. *What do we have here? I think it's time for...Katie! No, that sounds terrible. Slut Girl!*

With that Pandora leaped off the roof. Her wings flapped once behind her, slowing her descent. When her feet touched the pavement, both of the guys swung their guns in her direction.

Ooh, shit! This is great. She put her hands in the air.

One of the guys waved the gun at her, obviously not familiar with how to use it. "Stay back! This is none of your damn business!"

Pandora skipped toward them. "It doesn't look like you're being too nice to this gentleman. I don't like it, so I'm going to give you this one chance to put your guns away and make a run for it." Pandora waited for a beat, then shooed them away. "Go on, fucktards. Run away."

One of the guys pulled the trigger, and the report echoed off the alley's walls. Without even blinking, Pandora raised her hand and caught the bullet in her palm. "Hold on, hold on." The guys watched her, totally baffled. She dug her demonic claw into her palm and pulled the bullet out, flicking it at the shooter. The wound healed almost instantly.

Her eyes glowed bright red. "You had to go and do that, didn't you?"

Pandora moved faster than the guys could think, and suddenly she was on them. She grabbed both of their guns and ripped them out of their hands, then threw them up in the air. They clattered on a rooftop somewhere. "I gave you a chance, and now I'm going to fucking kill you."

Katie perked up. *Whoa, whoa, whoa! You're a vigilante. You don't kill the bad guys. You pick them up and take them to the police. Think Batman. How often does he kill anyone?*

Pandora sighed and rolled her eyes. *Fine.*

"Wha…wha…what the hell are you?" one of the guys asked. A dark piss-stain bloomed on his pant leg.

Pandora smirked and grabbed both of them by their shirts. "I'm your worst fucking nightmare, cock-gobblers. I'm Slut Girl."

She glanced at the older gentleman and gave him a nod. He was too shocked to respond. She leaped into the air and spread her wings, lugging the two would-be robbers out of the alley. She soared high over the city, the two men dangling by their shirts. She saw what she was looking for, and swooped down in front of a police station. Several cops were standing outside and they reacted quickly, putting their hands on their guns. A heartbeat later they realized who they were looking at.

Pandora threw the two guys on the ground. "Found these two twat gnomes trying to rob an old guy. Book them for robbery, or assault. Maybe elder abuse? They were armed, but I kind of threw the guns on a roof."

One of the cops stepped forward. "Aren't you Katie, from Katie's Killers?"

Pandora smirked. "Same tits, different eyes. Look up

here, sweet meat. And just so you know, I'll be around sometimes helping you guys get rid of the scum of the earth. When Katie's not fighting the hell out of demons, that is. You boys keep up the good work."

"Thanks, I guess?"

Pandora let her eyes sweep down the cop's body. "Give me a call sometime, boo. I'll give you a chance to blow my back out."

Katie groaned, so Pandora waved and took off. Katie was just along for the ride, listening to Pandora ramble and just letting her go with it.

I don't like dealing with the cops. I think from now on I'm just gonna beat the shit out of these guys.

Katie didn't even know what to say. *Fine, but no killing.*

Deal. You can do a lot to a human without actually killing them.

Pandora swooped down and skimmed the top of the shorter apartment complexes, listening closely. There was a park adjacent to one of the buildings, and she could see three men and one girl in the shadows. The guys were pulling on the girl's arm. She was obviously trying to fight them off, but she wasn't quite strong enough.

Pandora's eyes narrowed. She swooped down and came to a skipping stop on the ground, wings folding up behind her. She didn't even miss a beat, just walked straight over to one of the guys and tapped him on the shoulder. That got everyone's attention. The guys spun around, surprised to see Pandora standing there.

A big guy with a chin-strap chuckled and rubbed his hands together. "Lookee what we have here, boys." He blew a kiss to Pandora. "I like what you've done with that spandex."

Pandora growled at him. "Why don't you boys pick on somebody your own size?" She wiggled her pinky finger at them. "Or are you afraid of a real woman, you micro-penis motherfuckers?"

Chin-Strap snorted and shook his head. He stepped to Pandora and snarled, "You got a big mouth for a bitch."

Pandora kept an eye on the other two, but she inched closer to Chin-Strap. In a blur, she snapped her hand out and grabbed the guy by the throat. She pulled him in so close she could smell his fear, and her eyes flashed red. "I'm going to show you just how much of a bitch I can really be."

She slashed her claws across his face. He screamed, but Pandora was already picking him up. She body-slammed him onto the ground and spun to face the other two. One of the other guys pulled out a knife and lunged at her. Without looking, she swung her fist and connected with his temple. He stumbled backward and tumbled to the ground, unconscious. The last guy backed up and tried to run away, but Pandora wasn't having that.

She jumped into the air, and her wings snapped out behind her. She chased him across the park. As she got close to him, she tucked her wings and dove forward. Her claws snatched his ankles out from under him and they tumbled over one another until Pandora snapped her wings out, stopping them. She was straddling him, her claws at his throat.

He was frozen in place. She leaned down and put her lips just inches from his earlobe. "If I ever see you again, it won't be jail for you. I'm going to take you home to hell. I will do things to you that you can't even imagine."

Pandora grabbed his hair and slammed his head on the ground, knocking him out. She jumped up and waved at the terrified girl, still standing there. "You're welcome, sweetie. Have a good night!"

Katie sat at the breakfast table eating a plateful of eggs and bacon. She laughed as she recounted the events of the night before to Angie. "You should've seen the dude's face, not to mention the fact that he pissed himself right then and there. I would be mad that I had to clean my boots except it was so fucking hilarious."

Angie choked on her coffee, laughing. "So, it turns out that Pandora isn't too bad as a superhero after all?"

Katie shrugged her shoulders. "If we can figure out something better than 'Slut Girl.' Seriously, I can't deal with Slut Girl."

Pandora grumbled. *I tried Fuck Girl, but you said we couldn't yell that out in public.*

Katie ignored her, not even attempting to relay it to Angie. The night generally had been a success. She had saved about a dozen people from either thieves or rapists. She couldn't help but admit to herself that it felt good to do something for humankind other than killing demons.

Angie loved to hear the stories. "I still can't get over the guy who thought he could sweet-talk his way out of it with Pandora."

Katie laughed and was about to tell her how that had ended up when her phone rang. It was the general. She picked up the phone and walked over to the window. "Please tell me you killed the Leviathan."

The general scoffed. "I wish I had that kind of news for you. This bitch is turning out to be a bigger pain in the balls than I thought. I have good news and bad news. We found Tiamat swimming in the depths of the ocean. The bad news is, she seems to be heading in the general direction of the eastern US seaboard. I don't think I need to tell you why that's a bad thing."

Katie wasn't surprised. "Any idea where she's heading?"

The general chuckled. "I have a feeling you already know."

She's coming to New York. Our Big beautiful Apple, Pandora growled. *I'm pretty sure it's those cockholsters Moloch and Baal.*

Katie relayed that message as best she could. "Pandora thinks it's the two main demons, the fuckwits causing all the other problems."

The general pulled up the last email he'd gotten from the men working on Katie and Pandora's plan. "That doesn't surprise me at all. I received the clip of the smack talk we're going to use on the Leviathan to get her to come to the island. Here, I'll play it for you."

The general pressed play. "Tiamat, get your fish-fucking face over here. We're waiting for you. You think you're so big and bad? You're fucking *nothing*. Come out and face us! You're not even scary. You look like a mountain of pubes floating in the ocean."

Pandora cackled loudly and took over Katie's voice. "That shit is fucking hilarious! You don't tell a Leviathan thousands of years old she looks like a bush mountain. Here."

Pandora screeched out one sentence that neither the general nor Katie fully understood, then another. She made some very strange sounds come out of Katie's throat. Her words were a jumbled mess, a combination of English and demon.

Katie cupped her hand over her mouth, trying to stop Pandora from doing whatever it was that she was doing. "Oh, my God, Pandora. You sound like a fucking dying seal."

The general tried to hold back a chuckle. "We can't understand anything you're saying. It's not making any sense."

Pandora growled, "Fine, fuck you both in the ear holes. You guys just cannot hear nuance. Can you record something over the phone?"

The general typed on his computer for a moment and then responded, "Yes, if you can make it so at least the demon can understand it."

Pandora smirked. "Perfect. Press Record. Tiamat *esaeu xik ozz* fucking lizard. *Kaq esaeun* fucking scaled *ozz aewabbi sabbia oth moya ya juaar aem ya* Damned. *Gaer'q zota za fucking ztir esaeu ohiwa.*"

When Pandora stopped talking, the general pressed the stop button. "Okay, got it."

Pandora had lots more to say, but she figured that was a

good start. "Tell her that. Toss the speakers into the water and see if she takes the bait."

The general got nervous. "Aren't you going to be there?"

Pandora scoffed and shoved a bunch of bacon into Katie's mouth. "Why would we want to fight her? I'm a vigilante now. She's not even a demon. She's something else. She's probably killable. Well, that is a hypothesis at the moment. No one has ever killed a Leviathan. Fuck, she may be *un*killable. Yeah, you're fucked, and no amount of donuts is going to change that."

Katie just sat inside of Pandora, not jumping forward. The truth was, she really didn't want to do this. Katie knew that she could take care of the Leviathan if she really wanted to, at least she hoped that she could. On the other hand, if the beast could be killed by the military, she would rather leave it to them. It was a huge task to take on, and something she wasn't looking forward to it all.

Pandora could sense that the general wasn't exactly pleased. "No offense, but I've got enough going on trying to kill normal demons. I'm not too fond of being on an island when you guys start throwing around those big-dick A-bombs or whatever."

The general grunted. "Good point, maybe we let you sit this one out. We'll blow the bitch up the old-fashioned way."

Without giving Pandora a chance to say anything else, the general hung up the phone. Katie hoped beyond hope that Pandora had given him good information. *You think they will get her, Pandora?*

Pandora mused. *Maybe. I mean, perhaps she hasn't aged*

well, and she's ready to die? I'm sure her centuries of sleeping were just horrible.

You don't think they can do it, do you?

Pandora let out a cackle. *Hell, no. We need to enjoy our bacon right now. Mark my words, they are going to come back and ask us for help.*

Are you sure?

Pandora let out a deep sigh, realizing that she had to tell Katie the truth. *I'm sure. It was a heavenly host of angels that put her down the last time. You want to galaxy-size a can of whoop-ass, get a bunch of angry angels and let them really cut loose. The only reason she isn't dead is they didn't want to kill her. Bleeding heart liberals, every one of them. If I had been there, I would've cut her head off and sent her straight to hell. For some reason, angels have no problem killing each other—or killing humans, for that matter—but you put a giant lizard in front of them, they get all weepy-eyed. You would've thought that the angels created PETA.*

Katie didn't understand that, but then again, she wasn't a full angel. She just had angel powers. She had put down a lot of demons in her time and never had it crossed her mind to leave one alive. She couldn't even imagine standing in front of Tiamat and letting the beast go free. After all, you could see how well that worked the last time. Now there were hundreds of dead humans, and no angels to answer for it.

Katie punched at the bag hard. Sweat poured down her forehead. It had been a long time since she had been at the gym. She wanted to get some time in to get her body back in shape and improve her endurance. The more Pandora joined the fight, the less she was able to keep Katie's energy up, and that was really important during a battle.

She exhaled out of her mouth and breathed in through her nose. Her fists flew at the bag, one after the other. She followed the striking sequence her trainer had explained. He gave her tips on training as if she were a boxer, knowing full well she had no intention of getting in the ring. She had other battles to fight.

An hour after she got there, a couple of guys walked in. They weren't in training gear. They wore shirts decorated with both angel wings and devil horns. She recognized them immediately. They had been following her for weeks.

Katie ignored them and headed back to the changing room to shower. Several of the regulars gathered at the edge of the boxing ring. A bald boxer whispered, "You ever seen those guys before? They look like they're trying to sniff Katie out."

A boxer missing all but three teeth nodded. "I've seen them outside. They're fucking groupies."

The bald guy approached the groupies, flexing his arms to emphasize his point. "You don't belong here. This gym is by invitation only. We don't allow outsiders."

One of the groupies was taller than the other, and he looked down at the bald man. "Maybe we want to join. Get us one of those invitations. Unless the owner wants to tell us to leave, we're not going anywhere."

The bald guy brightened and clapped the tall groupie on the shoulder. "Oh, yeah? Okay. You want to be part of this gym, we gotta see your stuff. You gotta get in the ring to become one of us, the trusted twelve."

The members of the gym snickered as the two newbies got pumped up to become one of Katie's twelve. They thought they were tough boys from the Bronx, but it was obvious before they even stepped into the ring that they'd had zero training. It became even more obvious when they got inside and had their asses kicked six ways to Sunday.

The nearly toothless boxer beat each groupie to a bloody pulp. They ended the rounds hanging off the ropes, their face protection twisted all the way around.

The bald boxer rang the bell, then gestured to the battered groupies, letting the members know to get them out of there. The toothless boxer pulled the groupies to their feet. "Sorry, guys. I guess you need to work harder."

The two guys grumbled and stumbled toward the door. The twelve men stood around laughing until Katie came out, showered and ready. They all went back to working out, acting as if nothing ever happened. They were the twelve for a reason, and they didn't want to worry her with small stuff. They wanted her to feel comfortable and safe in the gym. It was one of the few places Katie could be herself.

Several sailors walked across the small island that they would be using to lure in the Leviathan. They were nearly through setting everything up. The only thing they had left to do was run an equipment check. They had to make sure the new system was properly functioning. There could be no problems and no distractions when it was time.

One of the sailors chuckled as he connected the cords. "We're going to catch the biggest fish of them all. The Navy's going for the Guinness World Record."

The sailors laughed. They knew this was a serious situation, but they were trying to keep the mood light. Another sailor shook his head. "I don't get it. Why don't we just nuke the bastard?"

"Where we gonna nuke her? We can't find her when she's out in the middle of the ocean because she's so deep. And when we do track her, she's too close to shore to stop. The whole point is to save the human race, not blow them up. Besides, with our luck, the bitch would catch it and throw it right back at us."

The sailors laughed, but it was forced. In some ways it was funny, but at the same time, none of them put anything past this new threat.

Tiamat swished her scale-covered tail, roiling the sea and scaring any fish in the area as far away as possible. She had been feeding out in the depths of the oceans, scooping up sharks and squid everywhere she went. The wounds on her sides were starting to heal, but she still wasn't at full strength.

The beast had followed the warmer current, enjoying that water and the prey she found there far more than the Arctic. She was on her way to New York, following an order sent by Moloch and Baal. As she swam, she began to slow down. She heard vibrations ripple through the water. The energy was familiar. It was something she had heard and sensed before, but not for a long time.

She changed directions and began to swim toward the surface, curious as to who or what was making that sound. As she breached the tumultuous surface, she could hear Pandora's voice coming from a small island across the water.

"Tiamat *esaeu xik ozz* fucking lizard. *Kaq esaeun* fucking scaled *ozz aewabbi sabbia oth moya ya juaar aem ya* Damned."

At first, Tiamat began to swim away. She was not interested in Lilith or her taunts.

"Gaer'q zota za fucking ztir esaeu ohiwa."

That last part stopped her. She looked back at the island, annoyed. The beast snarled and snorted air out of her nose, blowing bubbles in the waves. She was arguing with herself. Should she continue in the direction she was supposed to be traveling, or go after Lilith?

The voice came again. "Tiamat *esaeu xik ozz* fucking lizard."

That did it. She could no longer ignore Lilith. The Leviathan began swimming in the direction of the island.

Miles away, an aircraft carrier tracked the beast on its sonar. The captain of the ship watched as the beast appeared on screen. "Holy fuck! That bitch is huge."

Air support roared overhead, keeping their distance in case she was capable of taking them down. One of the pilots made a loop around and watched Tiamat move quickly through the water toward the island. "We have visual. It's like the Loch Ness Monster on fucking steroids."

Off to the side of the main island was another smaller island. Several sailors were at the ready, waiting to give the signal to fire. The sailors looked through their binoculars at the beast as it swam along, their mouths hanging open. They didn't say a word. They had been told the thing was huge and horrifying, but in real life, it was much, much worse.

One of the sailors stood up and dropped his binoculars

to his side. He could see the Leviathan fine without them. "I've never seen anything like that."

They watched as Tiamat slowly rose from the water. Scaly legs crept onto the shores of the island, and the Leviathan looked for her prey: Lilith.

***

The explosions could be heard for miles, and the roar of the fighter jets echoed across the water. Missiles shot from the planes, whined through the air, and slammed into the Leviathan's back. When they hit her hard-scaled body they exploded, cascading fire down her back and over her tail.

Still, she moved forward. She barely even noticed the planes attacking her. She lashed out with a claw and caught the wing of a plane flying too low. It swirled out of control, spiraling down into the ocean. The pilot ejected, and the wind caught his parachute. He never saw the strong green tail rushing at him. He was swatted out of the air like a fly.

One of the battleships fired a missile from their Aegis system and the missile struck the Leviathan in the back of the neck, enveloping her head in smoke and flames. She roared angrily and stopped dead in her tracks to look for the culprit. The fire from the planes might not have affected her, but the missiles coming from the ships were starting to piss her off.

The captain stood on the deck of the battleship, watching her reaction through his binoculars. "Give her everything we've got! Tell everyone to take this bitch down!"

As Katie walked from the kitchen back to the living room, there was a knock on the front door. She put her glass down carefully and stared at the door. She was on alert. Nobody had called to let her know she had a visitor. She opened the door with one fist cranked back, ready to fight.

The general put his hands up defensively. "Don't hit me. I come in peace."

Angie walked up, shocked. Not only was the general at her door, but the doorman had not called to let her know they had a visitor.

Katie sputtered for a moment, trying to get her wits about her. "I'm sorry. Come in, general. I'm just shocked to see you. Usually, the people downstairs let me know if someone is coming up."

The general walked in and took his hat off. "It helps to have a weapon and implore your doorman *not* to announce me. Sorry to be that way, but this is top-secret, and it's urgent."

Walking behind the general was one of his aides. Katie greeted her. This was one she hadn't met before, but at the same time, he had about a dozen working for him at all times. The general walked right into the living room. "May I use your TV?"

"Of course. What are we watching?"

Batman*!*

Not now.

The general took a disk out of his coat pocket and put it in the DVD player. "It's from the most recent assault on the Leviathan. It didn't go quite as we thought it would."

Katie watched the video, leaning forward with interest. The footage began from the air and showed the beast creeping through the water and making its way to the shoreline. Several jets were buzzing around, and there were a few battleships at the edge of the frame. As the video went on, missiles shot from the planes to slam into the beast. Explosions rocked the small island and fire, and smoke were everywhere.

Nothing seemed to be working until the battleships fired. When those missiles hit the Leviathan, flesh flew off in scaly chunks. The beast roared so fiercely that the trees on the island shook. Smoke clouded everything. The entire island looked as if it were going to crumble into the sea. The trees were on fire, and there were deep craters on the beach. Tiamat still stood.

Katie stuffed a handful a candy into her mouth as if she were watching a movie. "I hope nobody uses that island for summer vacation."

The general glanced at her. "If they didn't before, they will now. You know how crazy tourists can be."

Katie rolled her eyes. "The stupidity of humanity still baffles me sometimes. Sure, let's take little Jeannie and Bob on summer vacation! Let's go where the military bombed a giant lizard thing. We can take pictures of the beach, and the ocean, and with the pieces of rotting flesh and bone."

Pandora thought about that. *Sounds like a perfectly pleasant afternoon.*

The general snickered and popped some of the candy into his mouth. The aide stood by, waiting for instructions from the general. She was slightly taken aback by the way the two of them joked. It was her first time around Katie and Pandora, and she was having a hard time following them—not to mention the fact that she had never seen the general act so chummy toward anyone ever, especially not a demon.

They watched the video with bated breath. For several moments, the camera plane flew around but was unable to see what was below. The remnants of the missiles had left a thick fog over the entire place, but the planes were reluctant to fly any lower in case the beast tried to knock them out of the sky. The smoke began to clear, revealing Tiamat. She was beaten and bloodied from the attack, but still moving. She was leaving the island, lumbering back into the water.

Not a soul on the island made a movement. The only sound was the hum of the camera plane. Even the Leviathan was quiet, barely pulling her body down the sandy beach and into the surf. Blood streaked the sand behind her, but she kept moving. The Leviathan pushed into the safety of the waves. The last piece of the beast the camera saw was a torn and tattered tail, with some broken scales hanging off it as it slipped beneath the surface.

When the video was over, the room was silent for several moments. They were all trying to digest what they had just seen. The general had seen the video before, but the enormity of the battle still struck him hard.

Pandora immediately took over. "Oh, that's not good."

The general looked at Katie and lifted an eyebrow. "How much time before she heals?"

"My best guess? A month. You could hope for two months if she doesn't find enough food right away. Do they know where she is now?"

The general shook his head, frustrated. "They were able to keep up with her for a couple hundred miles, but then she went too deep. As soon as she does that, we lose her. When she resurfaces, it's hundreds or even thousands of miles away. She doesn't seem to have to come up for air or anything like that. She's been swimming too deep for our subs to follow. The pressure down there doesn't seem to bother her a bit."

Pandora put her hand on the general's shoulder and spoke to him like she was speaking to a child. "Remember what I told you. She is incredibly intelligent. She knows who did this to her. She also knows I wasn't on that island, because if I were she would have seen me. She may not have spent a lot of time around me, but also knows that the wife of Lucifer wouldn't call her to an island just to let the military take care of her. She saw every single one of you. She must have been stunned, because she didn't turn around and pulverize your ships. I'm going to go way out on a limb here and say you guys got incredibly lucky. The bitch gives zero fucks."

"She *saw* us?"

"She fucking saw you, buddy."

"And she knows who attacked her?"

"Yep. She's a motherfucker, but she's a smart motherfucker."

"Are you trying to tell me that the US of A just pissed off the Leviathan?"

Pandora chuckled. "You sure did."

Katie took back over. "Find her, and let's kill her. This has gone on long enough. I'm not willing to wait until she climbs up the Empire State Building and kills a bunch of people."

Pandora didn't see that coming. *Wait...what?*

Katie spoke out loud so she could include the general. "She's hurt now. We don't have a host of angels, just me and you, Pandora. That's going to have to be enough."

Pandora groaned. *Oh, that's a good plan.*

"We're going to kill the Leviathan, General."

We are so going to die. And we never even decided on a good costume.

The fleet moved through the water, coming from all directions throughout the Atlantic Ocean. From large speakers attached to their main decks, the sound of Pandora's voice speaking in demon blasted out across the water. They couldn't locate the beast on the sonar, so they hoped to draw her out from wherever she was hiding.

"Tiamat I *oz edizz* waiting *maen esaeu. Esaeu yor nur xuq esaeu yorraeq siga maenawabbi. Esaeu sowa qae yaeza ud zaeza-qiza, oth s'ar esaeu gae,* I *oz* going *qae qaon yoq* fucking *qoih aemm esaeun ozz.*"

Pandora's voice echoed, sending chills down the sailors' spines. This was the first time for many of them to be in direct contact with a demon, and it was a little bit over-whelming.

After hours of the ships cruising through the waters, something stirred far below the surface of the ocean. Mud cascaded. Alarmed fish swam in circles and finally shot away from the shifting seafloor. Even though the beast was foreign to the creatures of Earth, they knew danger when they saw it. The Leviathan took no prisoners and devoured everything in its path.

As the schools of fish swam quickly away, two eyes the size of pick-up trucks opened wide.

Katie looked out the window as the helicopter flew. She was being taken out to a new island, one that was all set up and ready for her. They made sure this one was also as far away from any inhabited place as they possibly could get. As she approached, she could see dozens of battleships in the distance. They stood off so as not to tempt Tiamat into swimming over to them and dragging them to the bottom of the ocean.

Katie knew that having any humans around was a bad idea. *These jokers are going to get themselves killed. I don't need any distractions right now. If I'm going to kill this bitch, I can't be looking after humans at the same time.*

Pandora took her usual nonchalant stance. *Hey, they know what the dangers are. If they want to be eaten by a giant sea-dragon, that's their business. You can't babysit everybody.*

You still don't get it. These people rely on me to keep them safe. They think that if they're with me, they'll be safe. They don't realize I can't protect all of them and myself at the same time. It's like the time we fought that demon in Times Square. People died because they expected me to save them, but I was fighting a fucking demon at the time. If I can do anything to avoid that situation, then I need to do it.

Pandora kept her mouth shut. She knew she wasn't going to change Katie's mind. If she was honest, Pandora didn't want to see anybody die either, but how often was a demon honest with anybody? Besides, she was completely focused on the giant beast that wanted to eat her whole.

Katie pulled her headset on and tapped the microphone to check it. "Can you hear me? Okay. I need everyone to back off. It's just going to be the Leviathan and me."

Pandora pouted. *Hey, and me! Don't forget about me! I'm here too.*

Katie chuckled. *I know, trust me. You don't let me forget those kinds of things.*

Katie stopped, realizing that sometimes, maybe she *did* forget that Pandora was there. She shouldn't do that. Pandora was very useful in these kinds of situations. Immediately, that gave her a new idea, one that she knew Pandora wasn't going to like very much.

As the thought passed through Katie's mind, Pandora could tell something was up. *What the fuck are you thinking?*

Katie began snickering, and Pandora didn't like it at all. *Why are you doing that? You sound horrible, like somebody butchering a pig.*

How much juice you got, you demonic bitch? Katie laughed.

Well, if you're gonna get me turned on by calling me dirty names, I got a lot of juice.

Katie obviously had something up her sleeve. *You got more in hell?*

Pandora sneered. *Of course. Oh, shit!*

The helicopter touched down and Katie jumped onto the shore. Before Pandora could ask her any more questions, a voice came over her walkie. "Be advised, Katie, the beast is eighty miles out and coming on strong."

"Roger that. I got this. Make sure you're back far enough. I can't protect everybody."

With that Katie took off the headset, and dropped it in the sand, not wanting anything to give away her position. She surveyed the area, looking for the best place to make a stand. It looked like an island from a television show. The center was densely wooded, surrounded on all sides by a white, sandy beach.

Katie kicked the sand with her boots. *If there weren't a Damned-eating monster heading my way I'd say this is the perfect place for a vacation.*

Pandora sniffed. *Too few men and not enough drinks. If you're going to drag me to the middle of nowhere, there'd better be something to entertain me.*

Katie climbed up the beach toward the wooded area. *I have a big old girl coming to visit you as we speak. I don't think she brought any umbrella drinks with her, but I promise she's going to be a good time. Hell, she* better *be a good time, because I'm just about done with this shit.*

Pandora giggled. *Sounds like a job for Slut Girl.*

Katie laughed loudly. *So, Slut Girl swings both ways?*

Actually, that would be like ten different ways. This is a lady, a fish-monster, and a giant scaled dinosaur.

Hey, I don't judge. If that's her thing, that's her thing—as long as by the end of it all that bitch is headed straight to hell.

Pandora narrowed her eyes. *Oh, I promise you this bitch has some serious shit to answer for.*

Great gouts of water shot up as Tiamat emerged from the sea. She looked around, snarling as she searched for humans and their flying machines. She flexed her cold, jagged talons, but didn't see any flying machines to swat.

The beast sniffed the air, surprised to find Lilith's scent. She followed it to the beach and slogged across the sand, her attention fixed on finding Katie and Pandora. She stepped to the edge of the beach and swung her tail, knocking down a stand of trees. The smell of her prey grew stronger.

Katie stood there, smiling widely. Tiamat howled and lashed out with her claws, but Katie was too fast. She darted away.

Lilith began to yell trash talk in Demon. "*Esaeu xik headed zaeyabbi* fucker. *Kaq esaeun ozz ud sabbia oth edaed* making *o* mess. *Gaer'q esaeu trael iqz nuga qae nux esaeun* fucking *qoih aewabbi zaezaaera ahza's xaokh? yoq's niksq* fucker, *iq's* Lilith *oth* I'm *sabbia qae* coochie *chq esaeu trael, esaeu're* fucking *gaera.*"

The beast smashed through the forest after her, tearing trees out of the sand roots and all. The battleships were videotaping the entire thing. Standing on the deck of an aircraft carrier was General Brushwood, holding his own video camera and getting as much as he could on tape. He wanted to be able to study the beast. Pandora said there were seven of them, and he wanted to be prepared. He didn't want to be stuck not knowing how to kill the fuckers next time around.

One of the sailors elbowed his buddy. "Do we know what she's saying?"

His buddy watched the general film, but nodded. "We've been studying it. I think we've made some headway on deciphering the language of the demons. I worked with several people at my last command doing that."

The sailor looked at him expectantly. "And? Can you tell at all what she's saying?"

His buddy pursed his lips, looking thoughtful. "Let's see. She called the monster a big-headed motherfucker, first of all. Then, something about her tail and dragging it all over someone else's property. I don't know what's next; it's not an exact science. Wait, she's saying something… She's about to kick her so hard her ancestors will feel it."

Suddenly, Tiamat spoke. Her voice was like a thousand windows being shattered at once. "*Esaeu doyaqiy gazaer*, I'll *qota esaeu oth esaeun* whore *liy za qae ya* depths *aem sazz*."

The sailors snapped their heads toward each other, surprised that the giant beast could speak. "What did she say?"

His buddy shrugged. "I think she just called Pandora a pathetic…"

Tiamat roared at the forest. She was beginning to realize that it wasn't worth her time to fight Pandora. She had a mission to accomplish, and she had been warned about how Katie and Pandora would try to draw her away. As she was about to go back to the sea, Katie jumped from the trees, her wings stretching wide behind her.

Tiamat bared her teeth and narrowed her eyes, letting out a furious roar. She smashed trees into splinters as she made her way toward the angel. Angel wings got the Leviathan every time. The angels were the ones who had defeated her before, and she wasn't going to put up with it a second time around.

Katie spread her arms out wide, closed her eyes, and whispered, "Sword and armor."

A flash of light shot across Katie as her body was contained in shining angelic armor and her sword snapped into her hand.

Katie half-expected Gabriel to appear, but no one came.

And the Leviathan was charging at her.

Pandora clicked her tongue. *Never an angel around when you really need him.*

Tiamat was gaining speed, getting her bulk going as fast as she possibly could. She lowered her head, ready to devour the little angel whole.

Katie bared her teeth and slashed. It surprised both the Leviathan and Pandora when the sword ripped reality and she opened a tall and powerful portal into hell.

Pandora whistled. *That's some pretty sweet shit.*

Katie chuckled. *I've got all kinds of surprises up my sleeve.*

With that, Katie made a running leap into the portal… and into hell. Tiamat's eyes opened wide as she put her feet out and tried to slow herself down, but it was too late. She was going too fast, and the portal was too close. The Leviathan roared, furious as she tumbled head over tail into the portal behind Katie.

She had no love for angels, but that didn't mean she wanted to go to hell. Especially alongside Katie and Pandora.

What neither of them realized was that the portal was shimmering as they moved through it. They didn't notice when the portal snapped shut behind them.

The general lowered the camera down and stared blankly at the island. Tiamat and Katie were gone. He couldn't believe his eyes. He hoped beyond hope that this wasn't the last time he ever saw Katie. He knew the last place that she wanted to be was in the depths of hell.

"**F**ucking hell! That was supposed to stay open," Katie shouted.

Pandora tsked. *Too much mass. If you had asked, I'd have warned you, but I think you have bigger things to worry about. And by bigger, I mean really fucking big.*

Katie looked up to see Tiamat charging at her. She let the beast come.

When she could smell Tiamat's stinking breath, she raised her sword. Tiamat's teeth flashed, reflecting the fires of hell.

Katie leaped out of the way, popped her wings out, and let them carry her up and over the Leviathan. She cut a deep groove in Tiamat's back with her angelic sword. The beast screamed and fell, rolling across the hardened lava .

Katie chuckled, but Pandora quickly pointed out that the Leviathan wasn't the only problem they were facing. *Looks like the demons are coming for you too. This was a fantastic fucking idea.*

"Shit," Katie groaned. The creatures scrambled toward her, snarling and spitting. She sliced her sword through the air, taking the heads off of two of the demons.

She was trying to stay alive, fight the Leviathan, and keep the demons back all at the same time, not to mention the fact that it was about a million degrees down there, which was very quickly draining her energy. Katie flew over the heads of two demons who lunged at her, then landed behind them and sliced them in half. She wiped the sweat from her forehead. She was exhausted already. *Can you open the portal again?*

And *keep you kicking ass?* Pandora blew out a puff of air. *I can't do both, baby.*

Katie narrowed her eyes and kicked a demon in the chest so hard that it sent him flying back into the depths of hell.

She held her sword with one hand and took a deep breath. With all her strength, Katie shoved her hand into her chest, pulling with an angel's strength.

When she ripped her hand free, it felt like she was tugging herself apart. But she was pulling Pandora free.

Katie dropped Pandora on the ground in front of her and the demon stood there in her full demon form, shocked. At first, Pandora's body shook, unused to being free. She had been stuck inside Katie for so long. Then she took a deep breath, reveling in the hellish air.

Katie leveled her sword at the demons charging her but spoke to Pandora. "Now's your time, Pandora. I've put all my faith in you. Save me, kill me, make me your angel bitch. It's up to you. What's it going to be?"

Pandora looked at her for a moment and began to cackle maniacally. A flash of panic ran through Katie. She was unsure what exactly Pandora was laughing at. Had she been played? Had she only pretended to care for Katie all this time to save herself?

Was Pandora really the demon Katie had tried to deny she was?

Pandora slowly craned her demon head toward Katie, her eyes bright in their sockets. "No one should ever, *ever* trust a demon, Katie. Especially not an angel."

Katie flinched as Pandora launched herself up, putting her snarling face in Katie's.

Katie gasped, ready for a fight. Instead, Pandora winked at her and kissed Katie's cheek. She lazily threw an arm up toward the demon horde attacking them and released a massive amount of dark, freezing energy. The icy black magic stormed through the air, laying waste to any demon in her sight.

The demons fell to the ground and burst into pieces, their bodies becoming wispy black smoke.

Pandora whispered, "Don't tell anyone, but you're my sister in word as well as deed."

Katie let a smile move across her lips. Pandora leaped up, unleashing her icy black death on more demons. Her demon body had transformed, and she was beyond beautiful. She was powerful and strong and everything that she had ever claimed to have been. Katie knew right then that she could always trust Pandora, even if she were outside their body. It was obvious that Pandora had been honest with Katie all along.

The demons decided they'd had enough. Instead of running full speed toward Katie and Pandora, they were now running as fast as they could in the opposite direction. Katie raised her sword. "I didn't even get to use this."

She laughed. "Fuck the angel sword. None of them want to mess with the Mistress of hell."

Behind them, Tiamat struggled to get to her feet. She huffed and puffed, struggling to breathe in the hot winds of hell.

"Hey, fish-face!"

The Leviathan turned toward the voice. Pandora was walking toward her, hellishly beautiful and beautifully hellish. "I hope you enjoyed stomping on the humans while it lasted. You're in my domain now, bitch!"

Tiamat let out a loud bellow, ready for a fight that never came. Instead of rushing the Leviathan, Pandora took a few steps back.

The demon queen extended her claws, black energy sparking around her. Nearby, Katie stuck her angelic sword in the rocky ground and leaned on it. The heat of hell was draining her, but she was resolute, not willing to give in. Still, she was weak.

Tiamat saw her chance. She howled with rage and ran for Katie.

Pandora chuckled and leaped for Katie. She grabbed her by the waist with one hand and pushed every ounce of dark energy she could in front of her. The dark stream sliced through reality itself. She had made a way out of hell, and she was taking Katie with her.

The Leviathan wasn't fast enough. She raced for them, but Pandora lifted Katie like they were newlyweds and leaped through the portal.

As soon as she felt the cool Earth air, Pandora slashed her claws in the air, closing the portal behind her. As the gate slammed shut, Pandora could hear Tiamat's bellow. She had been left behind, stuck in hell.

Pandora hit the ground with Katie, and she rolled across an asphalt road until a brick wall stopped them. Pandora cursed, then clawed at the wall in an attempt to pull herself to her feet. She wrapped her arms around her naked body, her tail covering her. They were in the same alley where they had saved a girl. That was a long time ago, it seemed, but it was fitting, considering that both of them were in pretty rough shape.

Everything had happened so fast. Pandora couldn't keep herself on her feet. She dropped back down on her knees and looked at Katie. Lying on the ground, Katie was unconscious.

Pandora weakly whispered, "Katie?"

Only a small groan came from the woman's lips. Pandora slapped her claws on the ground, gathering enough strength to crawl toward Katie. She was exhausted. The power she had in hell was gone, and the magic she had used was taking a toll on her body.

Pandora pulled herself over to Katie and leaned close to her face. "An angel should never trust a demon, Katie. But sisters always have each other."

Pandora closed her eyes and collapsed onto Katie. Her demonic body faded as she went back inside Katie.

Katie was alone in the alley, breathing quietly...and then not at all.

The only sound was the screech of a cat.

Then a cold wind moaned through the alley, and a moment later rain began to fall. A single drop of water plummeted between the buildings and splashed on Katie's head.

Katie gasped for air, and her eyes snapped open. They were redder than they had ever been before.

First, THANK YOU for not only reading this story but also reading through the back to our *Author Notes*, too!

I have a confession.

I can't seem to stop loving donuts (which wasn't a thing before I worked on PBTD and WOTD) and I have to blame my partners in crime on the *Protected by the Damned* Facebook group. It got so bad I threatened to create a character that loved Brussel sprouts, Keto diets and working out.

I hate all those items. Well, not so much the Keto diet (not that I am on it, but I've lost weight twice using that style of eating. It helps that I love meat.)

Everyone in the group seems to enjoy finding and displaying donut memes and damned if it doesn't make me salivate wanting another donut. I get them from time to time (the donuts), but the flavor rarely approaches the deliciousness of the images.

But, I'm not a quitter, so I'll try another donut in case it was that *last* donut I tried which failed me.

This book was a bit fun for me to work on, with the

whole massive beast and sending it to hell as a solution to get rid of it. I wanted to see what it would be like for Katie and Pandora to go back to hell, and how Pandora would react given the opportunity to reveal a secret plan and would she grab Katie and deliver her or is she who we think she is, and really has given those demons down below the finger?

While I can't make any promises, it seems that Katie and Pandora are staying on Earth…

For now.

Hope to see you in the next book, and if you have a moment, would you tell a friend or two about Pandora?

She would really appreciate it.

Ad Aeternitatem,

Michael

Yay! You made it to the author notes! As always, thank you so much for picking up a copy of book 5. I hope it made you laugh, cry, throw a few Cheetos? Maybe? No on the food throwing? All good.

The series has been a blast to be a part of. I know you guys have checked out the comic books Mike is working on for the series too, right? If not, you gotta jump on Facebook in the Protected by the Damned group and see these things.

They're beyond cool, and it's just like Mike to think outside the box. It's one of the best parts of working with him.

Well… summer is winding down. Only five more months of sweat your ass off heat for Texans. I can remember pacing the floor as a kid as October approached each year and summer was still in full effect.

What to wear on Halloween that you wouldn't risk passing out in as you collected your much deserved candy. I'd also try for dressing like a hooker (it's cooler like that), but my preacher mother wasn't having it. Too hot for the latest Halloween getup.

But I'm not in Texas right now. We're up in Kingston, New York and headed back up to Canada in a few days. It's not really that cool here either, but I'm loving the peace I'm finding in the little house we rented.

I'm thrilled to say that mine and Mike's 7Sons project should be coming online in September. We're wrapping up reviews and covers for the first four books in our Immortal Huntress line for the world. It's turned out to be quite a ride.

And on the *Damned* front, we're both busy working on Ella and Damien projects for this fall. I'm hoping we get to see the fruits of that storytelling next month as well. That's the plan at least.

Hope you're enjoying yourself in the series and in your life, wherever you might be. Summer is almost over, and fall is headed our way. Maybe. Depends on where in the world you are.

On that note, thanks again for stopping by the back of the book. I hope you reached this part because you finished the story. Even more than that? I hope you loved it.

Slave to Many Stories,
Laurie Starkey

PROTECTED BY THE DAMNED

Torn Asunder (01)

Killing Is My Business (02)

And Business Is Good (03)

Sit Down, Shut Up, And Pull The Trigger (04)

Welcome To The Jungle (05)

Metal Up Your Ass (06)

Dirty Deeds Done Dirt Cheap (07)

For Whom The Bell Tolls (08)

WAR OF THE DAMNED

Resurrection Of The Damned (01)

No Quarter (02)

Dark Is The Night (03)

Dim Glows The Horizon (04)

Waking The Leviathan (05)

www.ingramcontent.com/pod-product-compliance
Lightning Source LLC
Chambersburg PA
CBHW050241110726
47898CB00007B/2229